the soothing soak
a bathtub reader

stories

poems

essays

wisdom

the soothing soak
a bathtub reader

a
waterproof
book

MELCHER
MEDIA

Published by

 **MELCHER
MEDIA**

124 West 13th Street
New York, NY 10011
www.melcher.com

Publisher: Charles Melcher
Editor in Chief: Duncan Bock
Project Editor: Megan Worman
Publishing Manager: Bonnie Eldon
Production Director: Andrea Hirsh
Editorial Assistants: Lauren Nathan and Shoshana Thaler

Design by Elizabeth Van Itallie

08 07 06 05 04   10 9 8 7 6 5 4 3 2 1

Printed in China

ISBN: 0-9717935-5-7

Library of Congress Cataloging-in-Publication Data
The soothing soak : a bathtub reader.
p. cm.
"Project Editor: Megan Worman"—T.p. verso.
ISBN 0-9717935-5-7
1. Literature—Collections. I. Worman, Megan. II. Melcher
Media.
PN6014.S66 2004
808.8—dc22
2004010073

CONTENTS

Introduction

Our earliest sensation is blissful and serene, floating in the warm, protective bath of the womb. Is it any wonder that people in all cultures, from the beginning of history, have associated water with mystery and seduction, sensuality and spirituality, life and death? Rivers speak of journeys and time, of baptisms and great cities, of crossings into underworlds and the unknown. Oceans, with their awesome horizons and fathomless depths, whisper tantalizing, transfixing, and sometimes terrifying intimations of the infinite. Nearer at hand, we find the many pleasures of the bath. Moonlit hot springs, candlelit hot tubs, steamy Turkish baths, and the humble home bath. . . . Such destinations all promise a soothing escape. These are places for quiet socializing or solitary reflection. Places for rituals of purification or rebirth. Or for healing the wounded psyche.

In our previous anthologies, *Aqua Erotica* and *Wet,* we explored the erotic urges associated with water, gathering a variety of sexy, seductive stories involving aqueous encounters of many kinds. We visit new shores in this book: a selection of inspiring pieces of literature that trace the unmistakable connections between water and the human spirit. In these writings, water seems to carry the very filament of the soul. Whether set in, on, or near the water—or simply inspired by an idea of it—the stories, poems, and essays in this volume celebrate the transporting, transforming qualities of lakes, rivers, oceans, and rain. This collection is a true omnibus, with the feathery-light yet profound gestures of haiku masters Bashō and Issa standing alongside Andrea Lee's utterly contemporary short story about sexuality, race, and self-recognition on a Madagascar beach. In D. H. Lawrence's stunning tale, "Sun," a young mother attempts to reclaim her identity while sun-bathing on the Italian coast. And the spiritual philosopher Krishnamurti offers a haunting meditation on the mutability of life as symbolized by a river. Other pieces include authors as diverse as Elizabeth Bishop and Barry Lopez and settings as varied as the South of France and San Francisco.

It is no coincidence that water is tied to the spirit. We come from the water, and we return to the water, whether in sacred communion, relaxation, or wonder. Baths have become a sacred routine of our time. And this book promises to be the ultimate bather's companion—tranquil, revelatory, and uplifting.

—The Editors

The Woman Who Had Shells

Barry Lopez

The light is blinding. The vast, flat beaches of Sanibel caught in the Caribbean noon are fired with a white belligerence, shells lying in such profusion that people unfamiliar arrive believing no one has ever been here.

The shells draw July heat from the languid air, shells brittle as Belleek, hard as stove bolts, with blushing, fluted embouchures, a gamut of watercolor pinks and blues. Shivering iridescence rises from abalone nacre. Hieroglyphics climb the walls of slender cones in spiraling brown lines. Conchs have the heft of stones. One shell hides both fists; others could be swallowed without discomfort, like pills. A form of genuflection turned over in the hand becomes a form of containment, its thin pastels the colors to chalk a prairie sunrise.

Here at dusk one afternoon, thinking I was alone, I took off a pair of pants, a light shirt, my shoes and shorts and I lay down. On my back, arms outstretched, I probed the moist, cool surfaces beneath the sheet of white shells still holding the day's heat. I flexed and shifted against them until I lay half buried, as if floating in saltwater. The afternoon trailed from me. I was aware of a wisp of noise, like a waterfall muffled in deep woods. The pulse of my own heart faded and this sound magnified until in the mouths of the thousands of shells around and beneath me it became a wailing, a keening as disarming, as real, as sudden high winds at sea. It was into this moment—I remember opening my eyes suddenly to see flamingos overhead, their lugubrious flight etched against a lapis sky by the last shafts of light, the murmuring glow of pale crimson in their feathered bellies—into this moment that the woman stepped.

I turned my head to the side, ear pressed into the shells, and saw her first at a great distance. I was drawn to her immediately, to her tentative, cranelike movements, the reach of her hand. I imagined her fingers as polite as the waters of a slow and shallow creek, searching, sensitive even to the colors of shells, the trace of spirits. She was nearer now. With one movement she bent down and raised two shells, scallops, and cupped them to her cheeks. I saw clear in her face a look I have seen before only in the face of a friend who paints, when he has finished, when the mystery is established and accepted without explanation. I held that connection in my mind even as she turned away, knowing the chance these emotions were the same was only slight, so utterly different are human feelings, but believing we could, and do, live by such contrivance.

I wanted to speak out but could not move. She grew smaller,

touched one or two more places on the beach, like an albatross
trying to alight against a wind, took nothing and disappeared.

I stared across the white expanse into the vault of the
evening sky, toward emergence of the first stars. My respect for
her was without reason and profound. I lay for hours unable to
move. Whenever the urge to rise and dress welled up, a sense of
the density of the air, of one thought slipping irretrievably off
another into darkness overwhelmed me. When finally I stood,
I saw fields of shells around me luminescent in the starlight.
Near where my head had been was a single flamingo feather.
Across this landscape I made my way home.

We carry such people with us in an imaginary way, proof
against some undefined but irrefutable darkness in the world.
The nimbus of that moment remained with me for months.
That winter, on a beach frozen to stone I stood staring at the
pack ice of the Arctic Ocean. The gray sea ice gave way to gray
sky in such a way that no horizon could be found. In the feeble
light my breath rolled out, crystallized I knew on my eye-
brows, on the fur at the edge of my face. I wanted a memento.
With my heel I began to chip at the thin, wind-crusted snow
on the sand. There was a small shell, a blue and black mussel
barely the length of my fingernail. Stiff with the cold, I was

able only with great difficulty to maneuver it into a pocket of my parka, and to zip it shut. I was dimly aware at that moment of the woman, the turning of her skirt, extending her hand to the shells on Sanibel Island.

In one of the uncanny accidents by which life is shaped, I saw the woman the following year in New York. It was late in winter. I saw her through a window, reaching for her water glass in a restaurant on West 4th Street, that movement.

It was early in the evening, hardly anyone there. I crossed the room and asked if I might sit down. She did not move. The expression in her face was unreadable. I recounted, as respectful of her privacy as I could be, how I had first seen her. She smiled and nodded acquiescence. For a moment I was not sure it was the same woman. She seemed unveiled and unassuming.

She was a photographer, she said. She had been photographing in St. Petersburg when she went out that afternoon to Sanibel. I had been on vacation, I told her; I taught Asian history at the University of Washington—we found a common ground in Japan. A collection of her photographs of farms and rural life on the most northern island, Hokkaido, had just been published. I knew the book. In memory I saw images of cattle grazing in a swirling snowstorm, a weathered cart filled with a dimpled mound of grain, and birdlike hands gripping tools. In those first moments the images seemed a logical and graceful extension of her.

We talked for hours—about bumblebees and Cartier-Bresson, haiku, Tibet, and Western novels; and I asked if I could see her home. There was by then a warmth between us, but I could sense the edges of her privacy and would rather say good night, seal the evening here, hold that memory, than burden either of us. There is so much unfathomable in human beings; we so often intrude, meaning no harm, and injure for no reason. No, she said, she wouldn't mind at all.

We walked a great many blocks north, then east toward the river. There was ice on the sidewalks and we linked arms against it. Her apartment was a flat above weathered storefronts. We sat on a couch in a spacious room painted white, softly lit, with several large photographs on the wall, of seagrass and of trees in a field in Michigan. I had thought there would be shells somewhere in the room, but there were not that I saw.

I began looking through one of her published books, black-and-white photographs of rural Maine. She fixed a gentle tea, like chamomile. We sipped tea. She was very quiet and then she spoke about the shells. Whenever there was time, she said, she went out looking. When she was in Australia to work or in the

Philippines, or on the coast of Spain. When she first began she would collect them. Now it was rare that she ever brought one home, even though she continued to search, hoping especially to see a hypatian murex and other shells that she might never find, or find and leave. When she took vacations she used to go alone to exotic beaches on the Coral and South China seas, and to places like the Seychelles. Then, more and more, she stayed home, going to Block Island or Martha's Vineyard, to Assateague Island or to Padre Island in Texas, spending days looking at the simplest whelks and clams, noting how very subtly different they all were. The day I had seen her, she said, was one of the times she had gone to Sanibel to walk, to pick up a shell, turn it in the white tropical light, feel the cusps and lines, and set it back. As she described what she saw in the shells she seemed slowly to unfold. The movement of her hands to her teacup now had the same air of reticence, of holy retrieval and graceful placement that I had seen that day. She spoke of limpid waters, of unexpected colors, mikado yellow, cerulean blue, crimson flush, of their baroque and simple structure, their strength and fragility. Her voice was intimate, almost plaintive. When she stopped speaking it was very still.

The first pearling of light was visible on the window panes. After a long moment I walked quietly to where my coat lay and from a pocket took the small mussel shell from the Arctic coast.

I returned to her. I said in the most subdued voice I could find where the shell had come from, and what it meant because of that day on Sanibel Island, and that I wished her to have it. She took it. What was now in the room I had no wish to disturb.

I crossed the room again to get my coat. She followed. At the door where I thought to try to speak there was a gentle pressure on my arm and she led me to the room where she slept. Her bed was on the floor. Two windows looked east over the city. By the bed was a small white table with a glass top set over what had once been a type drawer. In its compartments were shells.

She slid back the sheet of glass and sitting there on her heels she began to show them to me. In response to a question, she would say where a shell was from or the circumstances under which she had found it. Some were so thin I could see the color of my skin through them. Others were so delicately tinged I had to be told their color. They felt like bone, like water-worn glass and raw silk. Patterns like African fabric and inscriptions of Chinese characters. Cone shells like Ming vases. She turned my hand palm up and deposited in its depression what I at first thought were grains of sand. As my eye became accustomed to them I saw they were shells, that each one bore in infinitesimal precision a sunburst of fluting. The last she lay in my hands was like an egg, as white as alabaster and as smooth, save that its back was so intricately carved that my eye foundered in the detail.

She put the shells back and carefully replaced the glass. There was a kind of silence in the room that arrives only at dawn. Light broke the edge of a building and entered the window, bringing a glow to the pale curve of her neck. In the wall steam pipes suddenly hammered. Her hair moved, as if in response to breath, and I saw the flush outline of her cheek. In that stillness I heard her step among the shells at Sanibel and heard the pounding of wings overhead and imagined it was possible to let go of a fundamental anguish.

from *Tao Te Ching*

LAO TZU

The supreme good is like water,

which nourishes all things without trying to.

It is content with the low places that people disdain.

Thus it is like the Tao.

In dwelling, live close to the ground.

In thinking, keep to the simple.

In conflict, be fair and generous.

In governing, don't try to control.

In work, do what you enjoy.

In family life, be completely present.

When you are content to be simply yourself

and don't compare or compete,

everybody will respect you.

Brothers and Sisters Around the World

ANDREA LEE

"I took them around the point toward Dzamandzar," Michel tells me. "Those two little whores. Just ten minutes. They asked me for a ride when I was down on the beach bailing out the Zodiac. It was rough and I went too fast on purpose. You should have seen their titties bounce!"

He tells me this in French, but with a carefree lewdness that could be Roman. He is, in fact, half Italian, product of the officially French no man's land where the Ligurian Alps touch the Massif Central. In love, like so many of his Mediterranean compatriots, with boats, with hot blue seas, with dusky women, with the steamy belt of tropics that girdles the earth. We live above Cannes, in Mougins, where it is always sunny, but on vacation we travel the world to get hotter and wilder. Islands are what Michel prefers: in Asia, Oceania, Africa, the Caribbean, it doesn't matter. Any place where the people are the color of different grades of coffee, and mangoes plop in mushy heaps on the ground, and the reef fish are brilliant as a box of new crayons. On vacation Michel sheds his manicured adman image and with innocent glee sets about turning himself into a Eurotrash version of Tarzan. Bronzed muscles well in evidence, shark's tooth on a leather thong, fishing knife stuck into the waist of a threadbare pareu, and a wispy sun-streaked ponytail that he tends painstakingly along with a chin crop of Hollywood stubble.

He loves me for a number of wrong reasons connected with his dreams of hot islands. It makes no difference to him that I grew up in Massachusetts, wearing L. L. Bean boots more often than sandals; after eight years of marriage, he doesn't seem to see that what gives strength to the spine of an American black woman, however exotic she appears, is a steely Protestant core. A core that in its absolutism is curiously cold and Nordic. The fact is that I'm not crazy about the tropics, but Michel doesn't want to acknowledge that. Mysteriously, we continue to get along. In fact, our marriage is surprisingly robust, though at the time of our wedding, my mother, my sister, and my girlfriends all gave it a year. I sometimes think the secret is that we don't know each other and never will. Both of us are lazy by nature, and that makes it convenient to hang on to the fantasies we conjured up back when we met in Milan: mine of the French gentleman-adventurer, and his of a pliant black goddess whose feelings accord with his. It's no surprise to me when Michel tries to share the ribald thoughts that run through the labyrinth of his Roman Catholic mind. He doubtless thought that I would get a kick out of hearing about his boat ride with a pair of African sluts.

Those girls have been sitting around watching us from under the mango tree since the day we rolled up from the airport to spend August in the house we borrowed from our friend Jean-Claude. Michel was driving Jean-Claude's car, a Citroën so rump-sprung from the unpaved roads that it moves like a tractor. Our four-year-old son, Lele, can drag his sneakers in red dust through the holes in the floor. The car smells of failure, like the house, which is built on an island off the northern coast of Madagascar, on a beach where a wide scalloped bay spreads like two blue wings, melting into the sky and the wild archipelago of lemur islands beyond. Behind the garden stretch fields of sugar-cane and groves of silvery, arthritic-looking ylang-ylang trees, whose flowers lend a tang of Africa to French perfume.

The house is low and long around a grandiose veranda, and was once whitewashed into an emblem of colonial vainglory; now the walls are the indeterminate color of damp, and the thinning palm thatch on the roof swarms with mice and geckos. It has a queenly housekeeper named Hadijah, whose perfect *pommes frites* and plates of crudités, like the dead bidet and dried-up tubes of Bain de Soleil in the bathroom, are monuments to Jean-Claude's ex-wife, who went back to Toulon after seeing a series of projects—a frozen-fish plant, a perfume company, a small luxury hotel—swallowed up in the calm fireworks of the sunsets. Madagascar is the perfect place for a white fool to lose his money,

Michel says. He and I enjoy the scent of dissolution in our borrowed home, fuck inventively in the big mildewed ironwood bed, sit in happiness in the sad, bottomed-out canvas chairs on the veranda after a day of spearfishing, watching our son race in and out of herds of humpbacked zebu cattle on the beach.

The only problem for me has been those girls. They're not really whores, just local girls who dance at the Bar Kariboo on Thursday nights and hang around the few French and Italian tourists, hoping to trade sex for a T-shirt, a hair clip. They don't know to want Ray-Bans yet; this is not the Caribbean.

I'm used to the women from the Comoros Islands who crowd onto the beach near the house, dressed up in gold bangles and earrings and their best lace-trimmed blouses. They clap and sing in circles for hours, jumping up to dance in pairs, wagging their backsides in tiny precise jerks, laughing and flashing gold teeth. They wrap themselves up in their good time in a way that intimidates me. And I've come to an understanding with the older women of the village, who come by to bring us our morning ration of zebu milk (we drink it boiled in coffee) or to barter with *rideaux Richelieu,* the beautiful muslin cutwork curtains that they embroider. They are intensely curious about me, *l'Américaine,* who looks not unlike one of them, but who dresses and speaks and acts like a foreign madame, and is clearly married to the white man, not just a casual concubine. They ask me for medicine, and if I weren't careful they would clean out my supply of Advil and Bimaxin. They go crazy over Lele, whom they call *bébé métis*— the mixed baby. I want to know all about them, their still eyes, their faces of varying colors that show both African and Indonesian blood, as I want to know everything about this primeval chunk of Africa floating in the Indian Ocean, with its bottle-shaped baobabs and strange tinkling music, the *sega,* which is said to carry traces of tunes from Irish sailors.

But the girls squatting under the mango tree stare hard at me whenever I sit out on the beach or walk down to the water to swim. Then they make loud comments in Malagasy, and burst out laughing. It's juvenile behavior, and I can't help sinking right down to their level and getting provoked. They're probably about eighteen years old, both good-looking; one with a flat brown face and the long straight shining hair that makes some Madagascar women resemble Polynesians; the other darker, with tiny features that belong to the coastal people called Merina, and a pile of kinky hair tinted reddish. Both are big-titted, as Michel pointed out, the merchandise spilling out of a pair of Nouvelles Frontières T-shirts that they must have got from a tour-group leader. Some days they have designs painted on their faces in yellow sulfur clay. They stare at me, and guffaw and stretch and give their breasts a competitive shake. Sometimes they hoot softly or whistle when I appear.

23

My policy has been to ignore them, but today they've taken a step ahead, got a rise, however ironic, out of my man. It's a little triumph. I didn't see the Zodiac ride, but through the bathroom window I saw them come back. I was shaving my legs—waxing never lasts long enough in the tropics. Squealing and laughing, they floundered out of the rubber dinghy, patting their hair, settling their T-shirts, retying the cloth around their waists. One of them blew her nose through her fingers into the shallow water. The other said something to Michel, and he laughed and patted her on the backside. Then, arrogantly as two Cleopatras, they strode across the hot sand and took up their crouch under the mango tree. A pair of brown *netsuke*. Waiting for my move.

So, finally, I act. Michel comes sauntering inside to tell me, and after he tells me I make a scene. He's completely taken aback; he's gotten spoiled since we've been married, used to my American cool, which can seem even cooler than French nonchalance. He thought I was going to react the way I used to when I was still modeling and he used to flirt with some of the girls I was working with, some of the bimbos who weren't serious about their careers. That is, that I was going to chuckle, display complicity, even excitement. Instead I yell, say he's damaged my prestige among the locals, say that things are different here. The words seem to be flowing up into my mouth from the ground beneath my feet. He's so surprised that he just stands there with his blue eyes round and his mouth a small *o* in the midst of that Indiana Jones stubble.

Then I hitch up my Soleiado bikini and march outside to the mango tree. "*Va-t'en!*" I hiss to Red Hair, who seems to be top girl of the duo. "Go away! *Ne parle plus avec mon homme!*"

The two of them scramble to their feet, but they don't seem to be going anywhere, so I slap the one with the straight hair. Except for once, when I was about ten, in a fight with my cousin Brenda, I don't believe I've ever seriously slapped anyone. This, on the scale of slaps, is half-assed, not hard. In that second of contact I feel the strange smoothness of her cheek and an instantaneous awareness that my hand is just as smooth. An electric current seems to connect them. A red light flickers in the depths of the girl's dark eyes, like a computer blinking on, and then, without saying anything to me, both girls scuttle off down the beach, talking loudly to each other and occasionally looking back at me. I make motions as if I'm shooing chickens. "*Allez-vous-en!*" I screech. Far off down the beach, they disappear into the palms.

Then I go out and stretch out in the water, which is like stretching out in blue air. I take off my bikini top and let the equatorial sun print my shadow on the white sand below, where small white fish graze. I feel suddenly calm, but at the same time my mind is working very fast. "My dear, who invited you to come halfway across the world and slap somebody?" I ask myself in the ultra-reasonable tones of my mother, the school guidance counselor. Suddenly I remember another summer on yet another island. This was in Indonesia, a few years ago, when we were exploring the back roads of one of the Moluccas. The driver was a local kid who didn't speak any language we spoke, and was clearly gay. A great-looking kid with light brown skin pitted with a few acne scars, and neat dreadlocks that would have looked stylish in Manhattan. A Princess Di T-shirt, and peeling red nail polish. When we stopped at a waterfall, and Michel the adventurer went off to climb the lava cliffs, I sat down on a flat rock with the driver, whipped out my beauty case, and painted his nails shocking pink. He jumped when I first grabbed his hand, but when he saw what I was up to he gave me a huge ecstatic grin and then closed his eyes. And there it was: paradise. The waterfall, the jungle, and that beautiful kid with his long fingers lying in my hand. It was Michel who made a fuss that time, jealous of something he couldn't even define. But I had the same feeling I do now, of acting on instinct and on target. The right act. At the right moment.

"Mama, what did you do?" Lele comes running up to me from where he has been squatting naked on the beach, playing with two small boys from the village. His legs and backside and little penis are covered with sand. I see the boys staring after him, one holding a toy they've been squabbling over: a rough wooden model of a truck, without wheels, tied with a piece of string to a stick. "Ismail says you hit a lady."

Word has already spread along the beach, which is like a stage where a different variety show goes on every hour of the day. The set acts are the tides, which determine the moves of fishing boats, pirogues, Zodiacs, and sailboats. There is always action on the sand: women walk up and down with bundles on their heads; bands of ragged children dig clams at low tide, or launch themselves into the waves at high tide to surf with a piece of old timber; yellow dogs chase chickens and fight over shrimp shells; palm branches crash down on corrugated-iron roofs; girls with lacy dresses and bare sandy shanks parade to Mass; the little mosque opens and shuts its creaky doors; boys play soccer, kicking a plastic water bottle; babies howl; sunburnt tourist couples argue and reconcile. Gossip flashes up and down with electronic swiftness.

I sit up in the water and grab Lele, and kiss him all over while he splashes and struggles to get away. "Yes, that's right," I tell him. It's the firm, didactic voice I use when we've turned off the Teletubbies videos and I am playing the ideal parent. "I did hit a lady," I say. "She needed hitting." I, the mother who instructs her cross-cultural child in tolerance and nonviolence. Lele has a picture book called *Brothers and Sisters Around the World,* full of illustrations of cookie-cutter figures of various colors holding hands across continents. All people belong to one family, it teaches. All oceans are the same ocean.

Michel, who has watched the whole scene, comes and tells me that in all his past visits to the island he's never seen anything like it. He's worried. The women fight among themselves, or they fight with their men for sleeping with the tourists, he says. But no foreign woman has ever got mixed up with them. He talks like an anthropologist about loss of face and vendetta. "We might get run out of here," he says nervously.

I tell him to relax, that absolutely nothing will happen. Where do I get this knowledge? It has sifted into me from the water, the air. So, as we planned, we go off spearfishing over by Nosy Komba, where the coral grows in big pastel poufs like furniture in a Hollywood bedroom of the fifties. We find a den of rock lobster and shoot two, and take them back to Jean-Claude's house for Hadijah to cook. Waiting for the lobster, we eat about fifty small oysters the size of mussels and shine flashlights over the beach in front of the veranda, which is crawling with crabs. Inside, Lele is snoring adenoidally under a mosquito net. The black sky above is alive with falling stars. Michel keeps looking at me and shaking his head.

Hadijah comes out bearing the lobster magnificently broiled with vanilla sauce. To say she has presence is an understatement. She got married when she was thirteen, and is now, after eight children, an important personage, the matriarch of a vast and prosperous island clan. She and I have gotten along fine ever since she realized that I wasn't going to horn in on her despotic rule over Jean-Claude's house, or say anything about the percentage she skims off the marketing money. She has a closely braided head and is as short and solid as a boulder—on the spectrum of Madagascar skin colors well toward the darkest. This evening she is showing off her wealth by wearing over her pareu a venerable Guns N' Roses T-shirt. She puts down the lobster, sets her hands on her hips, and looks at me, and my heart suddenly skips a beat. Hers, I realize, is the only opinion I care about. "Oh, Madame," she says, flashing me a wide smile and shaking her fingers indulgently, as if I'm a child who has been up to mischief. I begin breathing again. "Oh, Madame!"

"Madame has a quick temper," Michel says in a placating voice, and Hadijah throws her head back and laughs till the Guns N' Roses logo shimmies.

"She is right!" she exclaims. "*Madame a raison!* She's a good wife!"

Next morning our neighbor PierLuigi pulls up to the house in his dust-covered Renault pickup. PierLuigi is Italian, and back in Italy has a title and a castle. Here he lives in a bamboo hut when he is not away leading a shark-hunting safari to one of the wild islands a day's sail to the north. He is the real version of what Michel pretends to be: a walking, talking character from a boys' adventure tale, with a corrugated scar low down on one side where a hammerhead once snatched a mouthful.

The islanders respect him and bring their children to him for a worm cure he's devised from crushed papaya seeds. He can bargain down the tough Indian merchants in the market, and he sleeps with pretty tourists and island girls impartially. Nobody knows how many kids he has fathered on the island.

"I hear your wife is mixing in local politics," he calls from the truck to Michel, while looking me over with those shameless eyes that have gotten so many women in trouble. PierLuigi is sixty years old and has streaks of white in his hair, but he is still six feet four and the best-looking man I have ever seen in my life. "Brava," he says to me. "Good for you, my dear. The local young ladies very often need things put in perspective, but very few of our lovely visitors know how to do it on their own terms."

After he drives off, Michel looks at me with new respect. "I can't say you don't have guts," he says later. Then, "You really must be in love with me."

In the afternoon after our siesta, when I emerge onto the veranda from Jean-Claude's shuttered bedroom, massaging Phyto Plage into my hair, smelling on my skin the pleasant odor of sex, I see—as I somehow expected—that the two girls are back under the mango tree. I walk out onto the burning sand, squinting against the glare that makes every distant object a flat black silhouette, and approach them for the second time. I don't think that we're in for another round, yet I feel my knees take on a wary pugilistic springiness. But as I get close, the straight-haired girl says, *"Bonjour, Madame."*

The formal greeting conveys an odd intimacy. It is clear that we are breathing the same air, now, that we have taken each other's measure. Both girls look straight at me, no longer bridling. All three of us know perfectly well that the man—my European husband—was just an excuse, a playing field for our curiosity. The curiosity of sisters separated before birth and flung by the caprice of history half a world away from each other. Now in this troublesome way our connection has been established, and between my guilt and my dawning affection I suspect that I'll never get rid of these two. Already in my mind is forming an exasperating vision of the gifts I know I'll have to give them: lace underpants; Tampax; music cassettes; body lotion—all of them extracted from me with the tender ruthlessness of family members anywhere. And then what? What, after all these years, will there be to say? Well, the first thing to do is answer. *"Bonjour, Mesdemoiselles,"* I reply, in my politest voice.

And because I can't think of anything else, I smile and nod at them and walk into the water, which as always in the tropics is as warm as blood. The whole time I swim, the girls are silent, and they don't take their eyes off me.

Lazybones

PABLO NERUDA

TRANSLATED BY ALASTAIR REID

They will continue wandering,
these things of steel among the stars,
and worn-out men will still go up
to brutalize the placid moon.
There, they will found their pharmacies.

In this time of the swollen grape,
the wine begins to come to life
between the sea and the mountain ranges.

In Chile now, cherries are dancing,
the dark, secretive girls are singing,
and in guitars, water is shining.

The sun is touching every door
and making wonder of the wheat.

The first wine is pink in color,

is sweet with the sweetness of a child,

the second wine is able-bodied,

strong like the voice of a sailor,

the third wine is topaz, is

a poppy and a fire in one.

My house has both the sea and the earth,

my woman has great eyes

the color of wild hazelnut,

when night comes down, the sea

puts on a dress of white and green,

and later the moon in the spindrift foam

dreams like a sea-green girl.

I have no wish to change my planet.

The Infinite Passion of Expectation

GINA BERRIAULT

The girl and the elderly man descended the steep stairs to the channel's narrow beach and walked along by the water's edge. Several small fishing boats were moving out to sea, passing a freighter entering the bay, booms raised, a foreign name at her bow. His sturdy hiking boots came down flatly on the firm sand, the same way they came down on the trails of the mountain that he climbed, staff in hand, every Sunday. Up in his elegant neighborhood, on the cliff above the channel, he stamped along the sidewalks in the same way, his long, stiff legs attempting ease and flair. He appeared to feel no differences in the terrain. The day was cold, and every time the little transparent fans of water swept in and drew back, the wet sand mirrored a clear sky and the sun on its way down. He wore an overcoat, a cap, and a thick muffler, and, with his head high, his large, arched nose set into the currents of air from off the ocean, he described for her his fantasy of their honeymoon in Mexico.

He was jovial, he laughed his English laugh that was like a

bird's hooting, like a very sincere imitation of a laugh. If she married him, he said, she, so many years younger, could take a young lover and he would not protest. The psychologist was seventy-nine, but he allowed himself great expectations of love and other pleasures, and advised her to do the same. She always mocked herself for dreams, because to dream was to delude herself. She was a waitress and lived in a neighborhood of littered streets, where rusting cars stood unmoved for months. She brought him ten dollars each visit, sometimes more, sometimes less; he asked of her only a fee she could afford. Since she always looked downward in her own surroundings, avoiding the scene that might be all there was to her future, she could not look upward in his surroundings, resisting its dazzling diminishment of her. But out on these walks with him she tried looking up. It was what she had come to see him for—that he might reveal to her how to look up and around.

On their other walks and now, he told her about his life. She had only to ask, and he was off into memory, and memory took on a prophetic sound. His life seemed like a life expected and not yet lived, and it sounded that way because, within the overcoat, was a youth, someone always looking forward. The girl wondered if he were outstripping time, with his long stride and emphatic soles, and if his expectation of love and other pleasures served the same purpose. He was born in Pontefract, in England, a Roman name, meaning broken bridge. He had been a sick child, suffering from rheumatic fever. In his twenties he was a rector, and he and his first wife, emancipated from their time, each had a lover, and some very modern nights went on in the rectory. They traveled to Vienna to see what psychoanalysis was all about. Freud was ill and referred them to Rank, and as soon as introductions were over, his wife and Rank were lovers. "She divorced me," he said, "and had a child by that fellow. But since he wasn't the marrying kind, I gave his son my family name, and they came with me to America. She hallucinates her Otto," he told her. "Otto guides her to wise decisions."

The wife of his youth lived in a small town across the bay, and he often went over to work in her garden. Once, the girl passed her on the path, and the woman, going hastily to her car, stepped shyly aside like a country schoolteacher afraid of a student; and the girl, too, stepped sideways shyly, knowing, without ever having seen her, who she was, even though the woman—tall, broad-hipped, freckled, a gray braid fuzzed with amber wound around her head—failed to answer the description in the girl's imagination. Some days after, the girl encountered her again, in a dream, as she was years ago: a very slender young woman in a long white skirt, her amber hair to her waist, her eyes coal black with ardor.

On the way home through his neighborhood, he took her

hand and tucked it into the crook of his arm, and this gesture, by drawing her up against him, hindered her step and his and slowed them down. His house was Spanish style, common to that seaward section of San Francisco. Inside, everything was heavily antique—carven furniture and cloisonné vases and thin dusty Oriental carpets. With him lived the family that was to inherit his estate—friends who had moved in with him when his second wife died; but the atmosphere the family provided seemed, to the girl, a turnabout one, as if he were an adventurous uncle, long away and now come home to them at last, cheerily grateful, bearing a fortune. He had no children, he had no brother, and his only sister, older than he and unmarried, lived in a village in England and was in no need of an inheritance. For several months after the family moved in, the husband, who was an organist at the Episcopal church, gave piano lessons at home, and the innocent banality of repeated notes sounded from a far room while the psychologist sat in the study with his clients. A month ago the husband left, and everything grew quiet. Occasionally, the son was seen about the house—a high school track star, small and blond like his mother, impassive like his father, his legs usually bare.

The psychologist took off his overcoat and cap, left on his muffler, and went into his study. The girl was offered tea by the woman, and they sat down in a tête-à-tête position at a corner of the table. Now that the girl was a companion on his walks, the woman expected a womanly intimacy with her. They were going away for a week, she and her son, and would the girl please stay with the old man and take care of him? He couldn't even boil an egg or make a pot of tea, and two months ago he'd had a spell, he had fainted as he was climbing the stairs to bed. They were going to visit her sister in Kansas. She had composed a song about the loss of her husband's love, and she was taking the song to her sister. Her sister, she said, had a beautiful voice.

The sun over the woman's shoulder was like an accomplice's face, striking down the girl's resistance. And she heard herself confiding—"He asked me to marry him"—knowing that she would not and knowing why she had told the woman. Because to speculate about the possibility was to accept his esteem of her. At times it was necessary to grant the name of love to something less than love.

On the day the woman and her son left, the girl came half an hour before their departure. The woman, already wearing a coat and hat, led the way upstairs and opened, first, the door to the psychologist's bedroom. It seemed a trespass, entering that very small room, its space taken up by a mirrorless bureau and a bed of bird's-eye maple that appeared higher than most and was covered by a faded red quilt. On the bureau was a doily, a tin box of watercolors, a nautilus shell, and a shallow drawer from a cabinet, in which lay, under glass, several tiny bird's eggs of delicate tints. And pinned to the wallpaper were pages cut from magazines of another decade—the faces of young and wholesome beauties, girls with short, marcelled hair, cherry-red lips, plump cheeks, and little white collars. She had expected the faces of the mentors of his spirit, of Thoreau, of Gandhi, of the other great men whose words he quoted for her like passwords into the realm of wisdom.

The woman led the way across the hall and into the master bedroom. It was the woman's room and would be the girl's. A large, almost empty room, with a double bed no longer shared by her husband, a spindly dresser, a fireplace never used. It was as if a servant, or someone awaiting a more prosperous time, had moved into a room whose call for elegance she could not yet answer. The woman stood with her back to the narrow glass doors that led onto a balcony, her eyes the same cold blue of the winter sky in the row of panes.

"This house is ours," the woman said. "What's his is ours."

There was a cringe in the woman's body, so slight a cringe it would have gone unnoticed by the girl, but the open coat seemed hung upon a sudden emptiness. The girl was being told that the old man's fantasies were shaking the foundation of the house, of the son's future, and of the woman's own fantasies of an affluent old age. It was an accusation, and she chose not to answer it and not to ease the woman's fears. If she were to assure the woman that her desires had no bearing on anyone living in that house, her denial would seem untrue and go unheard, because the woman saw her now as the man saw her, a figure fortified by her youth and by her appeal and by her future, a time when all that she would want of life might come about.

Alone, she set her suitcase on a chair, refusing the drawer the woman had emptied and left open. The woman and her son were gone, after a flurry of banging doors and good-byes. Faintly, up through the floor, came the murmur of the two men in the study. A burst of emotion—the client's voice raised in anger or anguish and the psychologist's voice rising in order to calm. Silence again, the silence of the substantiality of the house and of the triumph of reason.

"We're both so thin," he said when he embraced her and they were alone, by the table set for supper. The remark was a jocular hint of intimacy to come. He poured a sweet blackberry wine, and was sipping the last of his second glass when she began to sip her first glass. "She offered herself to me," he said. "She came into my room not long after her husband left her. She had only her kimono on and it was open to her navel. She said she just wanted to say good night, but I knew what was on her mind. But she doesn't attract me. No." How lightly he told it.

41

She felt shame, hearing about the woman's secret dismissal.

After supper he went into his study with a client, and she left a note on the table, telling him she had gone to pick up something she had forgotten to bring. Roaming out into the night to avoid as long as possible the confrontation with the unknown person within his familiar person, she rode a street-car that went toward the ocean and, at the end of the line, remained in her seat while the motorman drank coffee from a thermos and read a newspaper. From over the sand dunes came the sound of heavy breakers. She gazed out into the dark, avoiding the reflection of her face in the glass, but after a time she turned toward it, because, half-dark and obscure, her face seemed to be enticing into itself a future of love and wisdom, like a future beauty.

By the time she returned to his neighborhood the lights were out in most of the houses. The leaves of the birch in his yard shone like gold in the light from his living room window; either he had left the lamps on for her and was upstairs, asleep, or he was in the living room, waiting for the turn of her key. He was lying on the sofa.

He sat up, very erect, curving his long, bony, graceful hands one upon the other on his crossed knees. "Now I know you," he said. "You are cold. You may never be able to love anyone and so you will never be loved."

In terror, trembling, she sat down in a chair distant from him. She believed that he had perceived a fatal flaw, at last. The present moment seemed a lifetime later, and all that she had wanted of herself, of life, had never come about, because of that fatal flaw.

"You can change, however," he said. "There's time enough to change. That's why I prefer to work with the young."

She went up the stairs and into her room, closing the door. She sat on the bed, unable to stop the trembling that became even more severe in the large, humble bedroom, unable to believe that he would resort to trickery, this man who had spent so many years revealing to others the trickery of their minds. She heard him in the hallway and in his room, fussing sounds, discordant with his familiar presence. He knocked, waited a moment, and opened the door.

He had removed his shirt, and the lamp shone on the smooth flesh of his long chest, on flesh made slack by the downward pull of age. He stood in the doorway, silent, awkward, as if preoccupied with more important matters than this muddled seduction.

"We ought at least to say good night," he said, and when she complied he remained where he was, and she knew that he wanted her to glance up again at his naked chest to see how young it appeared and how yearning. "My door remains open," he said, and left hers open.

She closed the door, undressed, and lay down, and in the dark the call within herself to respond to him flared up. She imagined herself leaving her bed and lying down beside him. But, lying alone, observing through the narrow panes the clusters of lights atop the dark mountains across the channel, she knew that the longing was not for him but for a life of love and wisdom. There was another way to prove that she was a loving woman, that there was no fatal flaw, and the other way was to give herself over to expectation, as to a passion.

Rising early, she found a note under her door. His handwriting was of many peaks, the aspiring style of a century ago. He likened her behavior to that of his first wife, way back before they were married, when she had tantalized him so frequently and always fled. It was a humorous, forgiving note, changing her into that other girl of sixty years ago. The weather was fair, he wrote, and he was off by early bus to his mountain across the bay, there to climb his trails, staff in hand and knapsack on his back. *And I still love you.*

That evening he was jovial again. He drank his blackberry wine at supper; sat with her on the sofa and read aloud from his collected essays, *Religion and Science in the Light of Psychoanalysis,* often closing the small, red leather book to repudiate the theories of his youth; gave her, as gifts, Kierkegaard's *Purity of Heart* and three novels of Conrad in leather bindings; and appeared again, briefly, at her door, his chest bare.

She went out again, a few nights later, to visit a friend, and he escorted her graciously to the door. "Come back any time you need to see me," he called after her. Puzzled, she turned on the path. The light from within the house shone around his dark figure in the rectangle of the open door. "But I live here for now," she called back, flapping her coat out on both sides to make herself more evident to him. "Of course! Of course! I forgot!" he laughed, stamping his foot, dismayed with himself. And she knew that her presence was not so intense a presence as they thought. It would not matter to him as the days went by, as the years left to him went by, that she had not come into his bed.

On the last night, before they went upstairs and after switching off the lamps, he stood at a distance from her, gazing down. "I am senile now, I think," he said. "I see signs of it. Landslides go on in there." The declaration in the dark, the shifting feet, the gazing down, all were disclosures of his fear that she might, on this last night, come to him at last.

The girl left the house early, before the woman and her son appeared. She looked for him through the house and found him at a window downstairs, almost obscured at first sight by the swath of the morning light in which he stood. With shaving brush in hand and a white linen hand towel around his neck, he was watching a flock of birds in branches close to the pane, birds so tiny she mistook them for fluttering leaves. He told her their name, speaking in a whisper toward the birds, his profile entranced as if by his whole life.

The girl never entered the house again, and she did not see him for a year. In that year she got along by remembering his words of wisdom, lifting her head again and again above deep waters to hear his voice. When she could not hear him anymore, she phoned him and they arranged to meet on the beach below his house. The only difference she could see, watching him from below, was that he descended the long stairs with more care, as if time were now underfoot. Other than that, he seemed the same. But as they talked, seated side by side on a rock, she saw that he had drawn back unto himself his life's expectations. They were way inside, and they required, now, no other person for their fulfillment.

Haiku

ISSA

TRANSLATED BY ROBERT HASS

Naked
on a naked horse
in pouring rain!

Napped half the day;
no one
punished me!

In spring rain
a pretty girl
yawning.

Story Water

RUMI

A story is like water
that you heat for your bath.

It takes messages between the fire
and your skin. It lets them meet,
and it cleans you!

Very few can sit down
in the middle of the fire itself
like a salamander or Abraham.
We need intermediaries.

A feeling of fullness comes,
but usually it takes some bread
to bring it.

Beauty surrounds us,
but usually we need to be walking
in a garden to know it.

The body itself is a screen
to shield and partially reveal
the light that's blazing
inside your presence.

Water, stories, the body,
all the things we do, are mediums
that hide and show what's hidden.

Study them,
and enjoy this being washed
with a secret we sometimes know,
and then not.

A Lamia in the Cévennes

A. S. BYATT

I n the mid-1980s Bernard Lycett-Kean decided that
Thatcher's Britain was uninhabitable, a land of dog-eat-
dog, lung-corroding ozone and floating money, of which
there was at once far too much and far too little. He sold his
West Hampstead flat and bought a small stone house on a
Cévenol hillside. He had three rooms, and a large barn, which he
weatherproofed, using it as a studio in winter and a storehouse in
summer. He did not know how he would take to solitude, and
laid in a large quantity of red wine, of which he drank a good
deal at first, and afterwards much less. He discovered that the
effect of the air and the light and the extremes of heat and cold
were enough, indeed too much, without alcohol. He stood on the
terrace in front of his house and battled with these things, with
mistral and tramontane and thunderbolts and howling clouds.
The Cévennes is a place of extreme weather. There were also days
of white heat, and days of yellow heat, and days of burning blue
heat. He produced some paintings of heat and light, with very
little else in them, and some other paintings of the small river
which ran along the foot of the steep, terraced hill on which his

house stood; these were dark green and dotted with the bright blue of the kingfisher and the electric blue of the dragonflies.

These paintings he packed in his van and took to London and sold for largish sums of the despised money. He went to his own Private View and found he had lost the habit of conversation. He stared and snorted. He was a big man, a burly man, his stare seemed aggressive when it was largely baffled. His old friends were annoyed. He himself found London just as rushing and evil-smelling and unreal as he had been imagining it. He hurried back to the Cévennes. With his earnings, he built himself a swimming-pool, where once there had been a patch of baked mud and a few bushes.

It is not quite right to say he built it. It was built by the Jardinerie Émeraude, two enterprising young men, who dug and lined and carried mud and monstrous stones, and built a humming power-house full of taps and pipes and a swirling cauldron of filter-sand. The pool was blue, a swimming-pool blue, lined with a glittering tile mosaic dolphin cavorting amiably in its depths, a dark blue dolphin with a pale blue eye. It was not a boring rectangular pool, but an irregular oval triangle, hugging the contour of the terrace on which it lay. It had a white stone rim, moulded to the hand, delightful to touch when it was hot in the sun.

The two young men were surprised that Bernard wanted it

blue. Blue was a little *moche,* they thought. People now were making pools steel-grey or emerald-green, or even dark wine-red. But Bernard's mind was full of blue dots now visible across the southern mountains when you travelled from Paris to Montpellier by air. It was a recalcitrant blue, a blue that asked to be painted by David Hockney. He felt something else could and must be done with that blue. It was a blue he needed to know and fight. His painting was combative painting. That blue, that amiable, non-natural aquamarine was different in the uncompromising mountains from what it was in Hollywood. There were no naked male backsides by his pool, no umbrellas, no tennis-courts. The river-water was somber and weedy, full of little shoals of needle-fishes and their shadows, of curling water-snakes and the triangular divisions of flow around pebbles and boulders. This mild blue, here, was to be seen in *that* terrain.

He swam more and more, trying to understand the blue, which was different when it was under the nose, ahead of the eyes, over and round the sweeping hands and the flickering toes and the groin and the armpits and the hairs of his chest, which held bubbles of air for a time. His shadow in the blue moved over a pale eggshell mosaic, a darker blue, with huge paddle-shaped hands. The light changed, and with it, everything. The best days were under racing cloud, when the aquamarine took on a cool grey tone, which was then chased back, or rolled away, by the flickering gold-in-blue of yellow light in liquid. In front of his prow or chin in the brightest lights moved a mesh of hexagonal threads, flashing rainbow colours, flashing liquid silver-gilt, with a hint of molten glass; on such days liquid fire, rosy and yellow and clear, ran across the dolphin, who lent it a thread of intense blue. But the surface could be a reflective plane, with the trees hanging in it, with two white diagonals where the aluminum steps entered. The shadows of the sides were a deeper blue but not a deep blue, a blue not reflective and yet lying flatly *under* reflections. The pool was deep, for the Émeraude young men envisaged much diving. The wind changed the surface, frilled and furred it, flecked it with diamond drops, shirred it and made a witless patchwork of its plane. His own motion changed the surface—the longer he swam, the more the glassy hills and valleys chopped and changed and ran back on each other.

Swimming was *volupté*—he used the French word, because of Matisse. *Luxe, calme et volupté*. Swimming was a strenuous battle with immense problems, of geometry, of chemistry, of apprehension, of style, of other colours. He put pots of petunias and geraniums near the pool. The bright hot pinks and purples were dangerous. They did something to that blue.

The stone was easy. Almost too blandly easy. He could paint chalky white and creamy sand and cool grey and paradoxical hot grey; he could understand the shadows in the high rough wall of monstrous cobblestones that bounded his land.

The problem was the sky. Swimming in one direction, he was headed towards a great rounded green mountain, thick with the bright yellow-green of dense chestnut trees, making a slightly innocent, simple arc against the sky. Whereas the other way, he swam towards crags, towards a bowl of bald crags, with a few pines and lines of dark shale. And against the green hump the blue sky was one blue, and against the bald stone another, even when for a brief few hours it was uniformly blue overhead, that rich blue, that cobalt, deep-washed blue of the South, which fought all the blues of the pool, all the green-tinged, duck-egg-tinged blues of the shifting water. But the sky had also its greenish days, and its powdery-hazed days, and its theatrical louring days, and none of these blues and whites and golds and ultramarines and faded washes harmonised in any way with the pool blues, though they all went through their changes and splendours in the same world, in which he and his shadow swam, in which he and his shadow stood in the sun and struggled to record them.

He muttered to himself. Why bother. Why does this *matter* so much. *What difference does it make to anything if I solve this blue and just start again. I could just sit down and drink wine. I could go and be useful in a cholera-camp in Colombia or*

Ethiopia. *Why bother to render the transparency in solid paint or air on a bit of board? I could just stop.*

He could not.

He tried oil paint and acrylic, watercolour and gouache, large designs and small plain planes and complicated juxtaposed planes. He tried trapping light on thick impasto and tried also glazing his surface flat and glossy, like seventeenth-century Dutch or Spanish paintings of silk. One of these almost pleased him, done at night, with the lights under the water and the dark round the stone, on an oval bit of board. But then he thought it was sentimental. He tried veils of watery blues on white in watercolour, he tried Matisse-like patches of blue and petunia—pool blue, sky blue, petunia—he tried Bonnard's mixtures of pastel and gouache.

His brain hurt, and his eyes stared, and he felt whipped by winds and dried by suns.

He was happy, in one of the ways human beings have found in which to be happy.

One day he got up as usual and as usual flung himself naked into the water to watch the dawn in the sky and the blue come out of the black and grey in the water.

There was a hissing in his ears, and a stench in his nostrils, perhaps a sulphurous stench, he was not sure; his eyes were sharp but his profession, with spirits and turpentine, had dulled his nostrils. As he moved through the sluggish surface he stirred up bubbles, which broke, foamed, frothed and crusted. He began to leave a trail of white, which reminded him of polluted rivers, of the waste-pipes of tanneries, of deserted mines. He came out rapidly and showered. He sent a fax to the Jardinerie Émeraude. What was Paradise is become the Infernal Pit. Where once I smelled lavender and salt, now I have a mephitic stench. What have you done to my water? Undo it, undo it. I cannot coexist with these exhalations. His French was more florid than his English. I am polluted, my work is polluted, *I cannot go on.* How could the two young men be brought to recognize the extent of the insult? He paced the terrace like an angry panther. The sickly smell crept like marsh-grass over the flower-pots, through the lavender bushes. An emerald-green van drew up, with a painted swimming-pool and a painted palm tree. Every time he saw the van, he was pleased and irritated that this commercial emerald-and-blue had found an exact balance for the difficult aquamarine without admitting any difficulty.

The young men ran along the edge of the pool, peering in, their muscular legs brown under their shorts, their plimsolls padding. The sun came up over the green hill and showed the plague-stricken water-skin, ashy and suppurating. It is all OK, said the young men, this is a product we put in to fight algae, not because you *have* algae, M. Bernard, but in case algae might appear, as a precaution. It will all be exhaled in a week or two, the mousse will go, the water will clear.

"Empty the pool," said Bernard. "*Now.* Empty it now. I will not coexist for two weeks with this vapour. Give me back my clean salty water. *This water is my life-work.* Empty it *now.*"

"It will take days to fill," said one young man, with a French acceptance of Bernard's desperation. "Also there is the question of the allocation of water, of how much you are permitted to take."

"We could fetch it up from the river," said the other. In French this is literally, we could draw it *in* the river, *puiser dans le ruisseau,* like fishing. "It will be cold, ice-cold from the Source, up the mountain," said the Émeraude young men.

"Do it," said Bernard. "Fill it from the river. I am an Englishman, I swim in the North Sea, I like cold water. Do it. *Now.*"

The young men ran up and down. They turned huge taps in the grey plastic pipes that debouched in the side of the mountain. The swimming-pool soughed and sighed and began, still sighing, to sink, whilst down below, on the hill-side, a frothing flood spread and laughed and pranced and curled and divided and swept into the river. Bernard stalked behind the young men, admonishing them. "Look at that froth. We are polluting the river."

"It is only two litres. It is perfectly safe. Everyone has it in his pool, M. Bernard. It is tried and tested, it is a product for *purifying water*." It is only you, his pleasant voice implied, who is pigheaded enough to insist on voiding it.

The pool became a pit. The mosaic sparkled a little in the sun, but it was a sad sight. It was a deep blue pit of an entirely unproblematic dull texture. Almost like a bathroom floor. The dolphin lost his movement and his fire, and his curvetting ripples, and became a stolid fish in two dimensions. Bernard peered in from the deep end and from the shallow end, and looked over the terrace wall at the hillside where froth was expiring on nettles and brambles. It took almost all day to empty and began to make sounds like a gigantic version of the bath-plug terrors of Bernard's infant dreams.

The two young men appeared carrying an immense boa-constrictor of heavy black plastic pipe, and an implement that looked like a torpedo, or a diver's oxygen pack. The mountainside was steep, and the river ran green and chuckling at its foot. Bernard stood and watched. The coil of pipe was uncoiled, the electricity was connected in his humming pumphouse, and a strange sound began, a regular boum-boum, like the beat of a giant heart, echoing off the green mountain. Water began to gush from the mouth of the pipe into the sad dry depths of his pool-pit. Where it tricked upwards, the mosaic took on a little life again, like crystals glinting.

"It will take all night to fill," said the young men. "But do not be afraid, even if the pool overflows, it will not come in your house, the slope is too steep, it will run away back to the river. And tomorrow we will come and regulate it and filter it and you may swim. But it will be very cold."

"*Tant pis*," said Bernard.

All night the black tube on the hillside wailed like a monstrous bullfrog, boum-boum, boum-boum. All the night the water rose, silent and powerful. Bernard could not sleep; he paced his terrace and watched the silver line creep up the sides of the pit, watched the greenish water sway. Finally he slept, and in the morning his world was awash with river-water, and the heart-beat machine was still howling on the river-bank, boum-boum, boum-boum. He watched a small fish skid and slide across his terrace, flow over the edge and slip in a stream of water down the hillside and back into the river. Everything smelt wet and lively, with no hint of sulphur and no clear smell of purified water. His friend Raymond Potter telephoned from London to say he might come on a visit; Bernard, who could not cope with visitors, was non-committal, and tried to describe his delicious flood as a minor disaster.

"You don't want river-water," said Raymond Potter. "What about liver-flukes and things, and bilharzia?"

"They don't have bilharzia in the Cévennes," said Bernard.

The Émeraude young men came and turned off the machine, which groaned, made a sipping sound and relapsed into silence. The water in the pool had a grassy depth it hadn't had. It was a lovely colour, a natural colour, a colour that harmonised with the hills, and it was not the problem Bernard was preoccupied with. It would clear, the young men assured him, once the filtration was working again.

Bernard went swimming in the green water. His body slipped into its usual movements. He looked down for his shadow and thought he saw out of the corner of his eye a swirling movement in the depths, a shadowy coiling. It would be strange, he said to himself, if there were a big snake down there, moving around. The dolphin was blue in green gloom. Bernard spread his arms and legs and floated. He heard a rippling sound of movement, turned his head, and found he was swimming alongside a yellow-green frog with a salmon patch on its cheek and another on its butt, the colour of the roes of scallops. It made vigorous thrusts with its hind legs, and vanished into the skimmer, from the mouth of which it peered out at Bernard. The underside of its throat beat, beat, cream-coloured. When it emerged, Bernard cupped his hands under its cool wet body and lifted it over the edge: it clung to his fingers with its own tiny fingers, and then went away, in long hops. Bernard went on swimming. There was still a kind of movement in the depths that was not his own.

This persisted for some days, although the young men set the filter in motion, tipped in sacks of white salt, and did indeed restore the aquamarine transparency, as promised. Now and then he saw a shadow that was not his, now and then something moved behind him; he felt the water swirl and tug. This did not alarm him, because he both believed and disbelieved his senses. He liked to imagine a snake. Bernard liked snakes. He liked the darting river-snakes, and the long silver-brown grass snakes who travelled the grasses beside the river.

Sometimes he swam at night, and it was at night that he first definitely saw the snake, only for a few moments, after he had switched on the underwater lights, which made the water look like turquoise milk. And there under the milk was something very large, something coiled in two intertwined figures of eight and like no snake he had ever seen, a velvety-black, it seemed, with long bars of crimson and peacock-eyed spots, gold, green, blue, mixed with silver moonshapes, all of which appeared to dim and brighten and breathe under the deep water. Bernard did not try to touch; he sat down cautiously and stared. He could see neither head nor tail; the form appeared to be a continuous coil like a Möbius strip. And the colours changed as he watched them: the gold and silver lit up and went out, like lamps, the eyes expanded and contracted, the bars and stripes flamed with electric vermilion and crimson and then changed to purple, to blue, to green, moving through the rainbow. He tried professionally to commit the forms and the colours to memory. He looked up for a moment at the night sky. The Plough hung very low, and the stars glittered white-gold in Orion's belt on thick midnight velvet. When he looked back, there was the pearly water, vacant.

Many men might have run roaring in terror; the courageous might have prodded with a pool-net, the extravagant might have reached for a shot-gun. What Bernard saw was a solution to his professional problem, at least a nocturnal solution. Between the night sky and the breathing, dissolving eyes and moons in the depths, the colour of the water was solved, dissolved, it became a medium to contain a darkness spangled with living colours. He went in and took notes in watercolour and gouache. He went out and stared and the pool was empty.

For several days he neither saw nor felt the snake. He tried to remember it, and to trace its markings into his pool-paintings, which became very tentative and watery. He swam even more than usual, invoking the creature from time to time. "Come back," he said to the pleasant blue depths, to the twisting coiling lines of rainbow light. "Come back, I need you."

And then, one day, when a thunderstorm was gathering behind the crest of the mountains, when the sky loured and the pool was unreflective, he felt the alien tug of the current again, and looked round quick, quick, to catch it. And there was a head, urging itself sinuously through the water beside his own, and there below his body coiled the miraculous black velvet rope or tube with its shimmering moons and stars, its peacock eyes, its crimson bands.

The head was a snake-head, diamond-shaped, half the size of his own head, swarthy and scaled, with a strange little crown of pale lights hanging above it like its own rainbow. He turned cautiously to look at it and saw that it had large eyes with fringed eyelashes, human eyes, very lustrous, very liquid, very black. He opened his mouth, swallowed water by accident, coughed. The creature watched him, and then opened its mouth, in turn, which was full of small, even, pearly human teeth. Between these protruded a flickering dark forked tongue, entirely serpentine. Bernard felt a prick of recognition. The creature sighed. It spoke. It spoke in Cévenol French, very sibilant, but comprehensible.

"I am so unhappy," it said.

"I am sorry," said Bernard stupidly, treading water. He felt the black coils slide against his naked legs, a tail tip across his private parts.

"You are a very beautiful man," said the snake in a languishing voice.

"You are a very beautiful snake," replied Bernard courteously, watching the absurd eyelashes dip and lift.

"I am not entirely a snake. I am an enchanted spirit, a Lamia. If you will kiss my mouth, I will become a most beautiful woman, and if you will marry me, I will be eternally faithful and gain an immortal soul. I will also bring you power, and riches, and knowledge you never dreamed of. But you must have faith in me."

Bernard turned over on his side, and floated, disentangling his brown legs from the twining coloured coils. The snake sighed.

"You do not believe me. You find my present form too loathsome to touch. I love you. I have watched you for months and I love and worship your every movement, your powerful body, your formidable brow, the movements of your hands when you paint. Never in all my thousands of years have I seen so perfect a male being. I will do anything for you—"

"Anything?"

"Oh, *anything*. Ask. Do not reject me."

"What I want," said Bernard, swimming towards the craggy end of the pool, with the snake stretched out behind him, "what I want, is to be able to paint your portrait, *as you are,* for certain reasons of my own, and because I find you very beautiful—if you would consent to remain here for a little time, as a snake— with all these amazing colours and lights—if I could paint you *in my pool*—just for a little time—"

"And then you will kiss me, and we will be married, and I shall have an immortal soul."

"Nobody nowadays believes in immortal souls," said Bernard.

"It does not matter if you believe in them or not," said the snake. "You have one and it will be horribly tormented if you break your pact with me."

Bernard did not point out that he had not made a pact, not having answered her request yes or no. He wanted quite desperately that she should remain in his pool, in her present form, until he had solved the colours, and was almost prepared for a Faustian damnation.

There followed a few weeks of hectic activity. The Lamia lingered agreeably in the pool, disposing herself whenever she was asked, under or on the water, in figures of three or six or eight or O, in spirals and tight coils. Bernard painted and swam and painted and swam. He swam less since he found the Lamia's wreathing flirtatiousness oppressive, though occasionally to encourage her, he stroked her sleek sides, or wound her tail round his arm or his arm round her tail. He never painted her head, which he found hideous and repulsive. Bernard liked snakes but he did not like women. The Lamia with female intuition began to sense his lack of enthusiasm for this aspect of her. "My teeth," she told him, "will be lovely in rosy lips, my eyes will be melting and mysterious in a human face. Kiss me, Bernard, and you will see."

"Not yet, not yet," said Bernard.

"I will not wait for ever," said the Lamia.

Bernard remembered where he had, so to speak, seen her before. He looked her up one evening in Keats, and there she was, teeth, eyelashes, frecklings, streaks and bars, sapphires, greens, amethyst and rubious-argent. He had always found the teeth and eyelashes repulsive and had supposed Keats was as usual piling excess on excess. Now he decided Keats must have seen one himself, or read someone who had, and felt the same mixture of aesthetic frenzy and repulsion. Mary Douglas, the anthropologist, says that *mixed* things, neither flesh nor fowl, so to speak, always excite repulsion and prohibition. The poor Lamia was a mess, as far as her head went. Her beseeching eyes were horrible. He looked up from his reading and saw her snake-face peering sadly in at the window, her halo shimmering, her teeth shining like pearls. He saw to his locks: he was not about to be accidentally kissed in his sleep. They were each other's prisoners, he and she. He would paint his painting and think how to escape.

The painting was getting somewhere. The snake-colours were a fourth term in the equation pool>sky>mountains-trees>paint. Their movement in the aquamarines linked and divided delectably, firing the neurones in Bernard's brain to greater and greater activity, and thus causing the Lamia to become sulkier and eventually duller and less brilliant.

"I am *so sad,* Bernard. I want to be a woman."

"You've had thousands of years already. Give me a few more days."

"You see how kind I am, when I am in pain."

What would have happened if Raymond Potter had not kept his word will never be known. Bernard had quite forgotten the liver-fluke conversation and Raymond's promised, or threatened, visit. But one day he heard wheels on his track, and saw Potter's dark red BMW creeping up its slope.

"Hide," he said to the Lamia. "Keep still. It's a dreadful Englishman of the fee-fi-fo-fum sort; he has a shouting voice, he *makes jokes,* he smokes cigars, he's bad news, *hide.*"

The Lamia slipped underwater in a flurry of bubbles like the Milky Way.

Raymond Potter came out of the car smiling and carried in a leg of wild boar and the ingredients of a *ratatouille,* a crate of red wine, and several bottles of *eau-de-vie Poire William.*

"Brought my own provisions. Show me the stove."

He cooked. They ate on the terrace, in the evening. Bernard did not switch on the lights in the pool and did not suggest that Raymond might swim. Raymond in fact did not like swimming; he was too fat to wish to be seen, and preferred eating and smoking. Both men drank rather a lot of red wine and then rather a lot of eau-de-vie. The smell of the mountains was laced with the smells of pork crackling and cigar smoke. Raymond peered drunkenly at Bernard's current painting. He pronounced it rather sinister, very striking, a bit weird, not quite usual, funny-coloured, a bit over the top? Looking at Bernard each time for a response and getting none, as Bernard, exhausted and a little drunk, was largely asleep. They went to bed, and Bernard woke in the night to realise he had not shut his bedroom window as he usually did; a shutter was banging. But he was unkissed and solitary; he slid back into unconsciousness.

The next morning Bernard was up first. He made coffee, he cycled to the village and bought croissants, bread and peaches, he laid the table on the terrace and poured heated milk into a blue and white jug. The pool lay flat and still, quietly and incompatibly shining at the quiet sky.

Raymond made rather a noise coming downstairs. This was because his arm was round a young woman with a great deal of hennaed black hair, who wore a garment of see-through cheesecloth from India which is sold in every southern French market. The garment was calf-length, clinging, with little shoulder-straps and dyed in a rather musty brownish-black, scattered with little round green spots like peas. It could have been a sundress or a nightdress; it was only too easy to see that the woman wore nothing at all underneath. The black triangle of her pubic hair swayed with her hips. Her breasts were large and thrusting, that was the word that sprang to Bernard's mind. The nipples stood out in the cheesecloth.

"This is Melanie," Raymond said, pulling out a chair for her. She flung back her hair with an actressy gesture of her hands and sat down gracefully, pulling the cheesecloth round her knees and staring down at her ankles. She had long pale hairless legs with very pretty feet. Her toenails were varnished with a pink pearly varnish. She turned them this way and that, admiring them. She wore rather a lot of very pink lipstick and smiled in a satisfied way at her own toes.

"Do you want coffee?" Bernard said to Melanie.

"She doesn't speak English," said Raymond. He leaned over and made a guzzling, kissing noise in the hollow of her collarbone. "Do you, darling?"

He was obviously going to make no attempt to explain her presence. It was not even quite clear that he knew that Bernard had a right to an explanation, or that he had himself any idea where she had come from. He was simply obsessed. His fingers were pulled towards her hair like needles to a magnet: he kept standing up and kissing her breasts, her shoulders, her ears. Bernard watched Raymond's fat tongue explore the coil of Melanie's ear with considerable distaste.

"Will you have coffee?" he said to Melanie in French. He indicated the coffee pot. She bent her head towards it with a quick curving movement, sniffed it, and then hovered briefly over the milk jug.

"This," she said, indicating the hot milk. "I will drink this."

She looked at Bernard with huge black eyes under long lashes.

"I wish you joy," said Bernard in Cévenol French, "of your immortal soul."

"Hey," said Raymond, "don't flirt with my girl in foreign languages."

"I don't flirt," said Bernard. "I paint."

"And we'll be off after breakfast and leave you to your painting," said Raymond. "Won't we, my sweet darling? Melanie wants—Melanie hasn't got—she didn't exactly bring—you understand—all her clothes and things. We're going to Cannes and buy some real clothes. Melanie wants to see the film festival and the stars. You won't mind, old friend, you didn't want me in the first place. I don't want to interrupt your *painting. Chacun à sa boue,* as we used to say in the army, I know that much French."

Melanie held out her pretty fat hands and turned them over and over with considerable satisfaction. They were pinkly pale and also ornamented with pearly nail-varnish. She did not look at Raymond, simply twisted her head about with what could have been pleasure at his little sallies of physical attention, or could have been irritation. She did not speak. She smiled a little, over her milk, like a satisfied cat, displaying two rows of sweet little pearly teeth between her glossy pink lips.

Raymond's packing did not take long. Melanie turned out to have one piece of luggage—a large green leather bag full of rattling coins, by the sound. Raymond saw her into the car like a princess, and came back to say goodbye to his friend.

"Have a good time," said Bernard. "Beware of philosophers."

"Where would I find any philosophers?" asked Raymond, who had done theatre design at art school with Bernard and now designed sets for a successful children's TV programme called *The A-Mazing Maze of Monsters*. "Philosophers are extinct. I think your wits are turning, old friend, with stomping around on your own. You need a girlfriend."

"I don't," said Bernard. "Have a good holiday."

"We're going to be married," said Raymond, looking surprised, as though he himself had not known this until he said it. The face of Melanie swam at the car window, the pearly teeth visible inside the soft lips, the dark eyes staring. "I must go," said Raymond. "Melanie's waiting."

Left to himself, Bernard settled back into the bliss of solitude. He looked at his latest work and saw that it was good. Encouraged, he looked at his earlier work and saw that that was good, too. All those blues, all those curious questions, all those almost-answers. The only problem was, where to go now. He walked up and down, he remembered the philosopher and laughed. He got out his Keats. He reread the dreadful moment in *Lamia* where the bride vanished away under the coldly malevolent eye of the sage.

Do not all charms fly
At the mere touch of cold philosophy?
There was an awful rainbow once in heaven:
We know her woof, her texture; she is given
In the dull catalogue of common things.
Philosophy will clip an Angel's wings,
Conquer all mysteries by rule and line,
Empty the haunted air and gnomed mine—
Unweave a rainbow, as it erewhile made
The tender-personed Lamia melt into a shade.

Personally, Bernard said to himself, he had never gone along with Keats about all that stuff. By philosophy Keats seems to mean natural science, and personally he, Bernard, would rather have the optical mysteries of waves and particles in the water and light of the rainbow than any old gnome or fay. He had been at least as interested in the problems of reflection and refraction when he had the lovely snake in his pool as he had been in its oddity—in its *otherness*—as snakes went. He hoped that no natural scientist would come along and find Melanie's blood group to be that of some sort of herpes, or do an X-ray and see something odd in her spine. She made a very good blowzy sort of a woman, just right for Raymond. He wondered what sort of a woman she would have become for him, and dismissed the problem. He didn't want a woman. He wanted another visual idea. A mystery to be explained by rule and line. He looked around his breakfast table. A rather nondescript orange-brown butterfly was sipping the juice of the rejected peaches. It had a golden eye at the base of its wings and a rather lovely white streak, shaped like a tiny dragon-wing. It stood on the glistening rich yellow peach-flesh and manoeuvred its body to sip the sugary juices and suddenly it was not orange-brown at all, it was a rich, gleaming intense purple. And then it was both at once, orange-gold and purple-veiled, and then it was purple again, and then it folded its wings and the undersides had a purple eye and a soft green streak, and tan, and white edged with charcoal . . .

When he came back with his paintbox it was still turning and sipping. He mixed purple, he mixed orange, he made browns. It was done with a dusting of scales, with refractions of rays. The pigments were discovered and measured, the scales on the wings were noted and *seen,* everything was a mystery, serpents and water and light. He was off again. Exact study would not clip this creature's wings, it would dazzle his eyes with its brightness. Don't go, he begged it, watching and learning, don't go. Purple and orange is a terrible and violent fate. There is months of work in it. Bernard attacked it. He was happy, in one of the ways in which human beings are happy.

Pleasure Seas

ELIZABETH BISHOP

In the walled off swimming-pool the water is perfectly flat.

The pink Seurat bathers are dipping themselves in and out

Through a pane of bluish glass.

The cloud reflections pass

Huge amoeba-motions directly through

The beds of bathing caps: white, lavender, and blue.

If the sky turns gray, the water turns opaque,

Pistachio green and Mermaid Milk.

But out among the keys

Where the water goes its own way, the shallow pleasure seas

Drift this way and that mingling currents and tides

In most of the colors that swarm around the sides

Of soap-bubbles, poisonous and fabulous.

And the keys float lightly like rolls of green dust.

From an airplane the water's heavy sheet

Of glass above a bas-relief:

Clay-yellow coral and purple dulces

And long, leaning, submerged green grass.

Across it a wide shadow pulses.

The water is a burning-glass

Turned to the sun

That blues and cools as the afternoon wears on,

And liquidly

Floats weeds, surrounds fish, supports a violently red bell-buoy

Whose neon-color vibrates over it, whose bells vibrate

Through it. It glitters rhythmically

To shock after shock of electricity.

The sea is delight. The sea means *room*.

It is a dance-floor, a well ventilated ballroom.

From the swimming-pool or from the deck of a ship

Pleasures strike off humming, and skip

Over the tinsel surface: a Grief floats off

Spreading out thin like oil. And Love

Sets out determinedly in a straight line,

One of his burning ideas in mind,

Keeping his eyes on

The bright horizon,

But shatters immediately, suffers refraction,

And comes back in shoals of distraction.

Happy the people in the swimming-pool and on the yacht,

Happy the man in that airplane, likely as not—

And out there where the coral reef is a shelf

The water runs at it, leaps, throws itself

Lightly, lightly, whitening in the air:

An acre of cold white spray is there

Dancing happily by itself.

The River of Life
from *Think on These Things*

KRISHNAMURTI

I don't know if on your walks you have noticed a long, narrow pool beside the river. Some fishermen must have dug it, and it is not connected with the river. The river is flowing steadily, deep and wide, but this pool is heavy with scum because it is not connected with the life of the river, and there are no fish in it. It is a stagnant pool, and the deep river, full of life and vitality, flows swiftly along.

Now, don't you think human beings are like that? They dig a little pool for themselves away from the swift current of life, and in that little pool they stagnate, die; and this stagnation, this decay we call existence. That is, we all want a state of permanency; we want certain desires to last for ever, we want pleasures to have no end. We dig a little hole and barricade ourselves in it with our families, with our ambitions, our cultures, our fears, our gods, our various forms of worship, and there we die, letting life go by—that life which is impermanent, constantly changing, which is so swift, which has such enormous depths, such extraordinary vitality and beauty.

Have you not noticed that if you sit quietly on the bank of the river you hear its song—the lapping of water, the sound of the current going by? There is always a sense of movement, an extraordinary movement towards the wider and the deeper. But in the little pool there is no movement at all, its water is stagnant. And if you observe you will see that this is what most of us want: little stagnant pools of existence away from life. We say that our pool-existence is right, and we have invented a philosophy to justify it; we have developed social, political, economic and religious theories in support of it, and we don't want to be disturbed because, you see, what we are after is a sense of permanency.

Do you know what it means to seek permanency? It means wanting the pleasurable to continue indefinitely, and wanting that which is not pleasurable to end as quickly as possible. We want the name that we bear to be known and to continue through family, through property. We want a sense of permanency in our relationships, in our activities, which means that we are seeking a lasting, continuous life in the stagnant pool; we don't want any real changes there, so we have built a society which guarantees us the permanency of property, of name, of fame.

But you see, life is not like that at all; life is not permanent. Like the leaves that fall from a tree, all things are impermanent, nothing endures; there is always change and death. Have you ever noticed a tree standing naked against the sky, how beautiful it is? All its branches are outlined, and in its nakedness there is a poem, there is a song. Every leaf is gone and it is waiting for the spring. When the spring comes it again fills the tree with the music of many leaves, which in due season fall and are blown away; and that is the way of life.

But we don't want anything of that kind. We cling to our children, to our traditions, to our society, to our names and our little virtues, because we want permanency; and that is why we are afraid to die. We are afraid to lose the things we know. But life is not what we would like it to be; life is not permanent at all. Birds die, snow melts away, trees are cut down or destroyed by storms, and so on. But we want everything that gives us satisfaction to be permanent; we want our position, the authority we have over people, to endure. We refuse to accept life as it is in fact.

The fact is that life is like the river: endlessly moving on, ever seeking, exploring, pushing, overflowing its banks, penetrating every crevice with its water. But, you see, the mind won't allow that happen to itself. The mind sees that it is dangerous, risky to live in a state of impermanency, insecurity, so it builds a wall around itself; the wall of tradition, of organized religion, of political and social theories. Family, name, property, the little virtues that we have cultivated—these are all within the walls, away from life. Life is moving, impermanent, and it ceaselessly tries to penetrate, to break down these walls, behind which there is a confusion and misery. The gods within the walls are all false gods, and their writings and philosophies have no meaning because life is beyond them.

Now, a mind that has no walls, that is not burdened with its own acquisitions, accumulations, with its own knowledge, a mind that lives timelessly, insecurely—to such a mind, life is an extraordinary thing. Such a mind is life itself, because life has no resting place. But most of us want a resting place; we want a little house, a name, a position, and we say these things are very important. We demand permanency and create a culture based on this demand, inventing gods which are not gods at all but merely a projection of our own desires.

A mind which is seeking permanency soon stagnates; like that pool along the river, it is soon full of corruption, decay. Only the mind which has no walls, no foothold, no barrier, no resting place, which is moving completely with life, timelessly pushing on, exploring, exploding—only such a mind can be happy, eternally new, because it is creative in itself.

Do you understand what I am talking about? You should, because all this is part of real education and, when you understand it, your whole life will be transformed, your relationship with the world, with your neighbor, with your wife or husband, will have a totally different meaning. Then you won't try to fulfil yourself through anything, seeing that the pursuit of fulfilment only invites sorrow and misery. That is why you should ask your teachers about all this and discuss it among yourselves. If you understand it, you will have begun to understand the extraordinary truth of what life is, and in that understanding there is great beauty and love, the flowering of goodness. But the efforts of a mind that is seeking a pool of security, or permanency, can only lead to darkness and corruption. Once established in the pool, such a mind is afraid to venture out, to seek, to explore; but truth, God, reality or what you will, lies beyond the pool.

Do you know what religion is? It is not in the chant, it is not in the performance of *puja,* or any other ritual, it is not in the worship of tin gods or stone images, it is not in the temples and churches, it is not in the reading of the Bible or the *Gita,* it is not in the repeating of a sacred name or in the following of some other superstition invented by men. None of this is religion.

Religion is the feeling of goodness, that love which is like the river, living, moving everlastingly. In that state you will find there comes a moment when there is no longer any search at all; and this ending of search is the beginning of something totally different. The search for God, for truth, the feeling of being completely good—not the cultivation of goodness, of humility, but the seeking out of something beyond the inventions and tricks of the mind, which means having a feeling for that something, living in it, being it—*that* is true religion. But you can do that only when you leave the pool you have dug for yourself and go out into the river of life. Then life has an astonishing way of taking care of you, because then there is no taking care on your part. Life carries you where it will because you are part of itself; then there is no problem of security, of what people say or don't say, and that is the beauty of life.

Neither Out Far Nor In Deep

ROBERT FROST

The people along the sand
All turn and look one way.
They turn their back on the land.
They look at the sea all day.

As long as it takes to pass
A ship keeps raising its hull;
The wetter ground like glass
Reflects a standing gull.

The land may vary more;
But wherever the truth may be—
The water comes ashore,
And the people look at the sea.

They cannot look out far.
They cannot look in deep.
But when was that ever a bar
To any watch they keep?

The Smoothest Way Is Full of Stones

JULIE ORRINGER

We aren't supposed to be swimming at all. It is Friday afternoon, and we're supposed to be bringing groceries home to Esty's mother so she can prepare Shabbos dinner. But it's the middle of July, and heat radiates from every leaf and blade of grass along the lake road, from the tar-papered sides of the lake cottages, from the dust that hangs in the air like sheer curtains. We throw our bikes into the shade behind the Perelmans' shed, take off our socks and shoes, and run through warm grass down to their slip of private beach, trespassing, unafraid of getting caught, because old Mr. and Mrs. Perelman won't arrive at their cottage until August, according to my cousin. Esty and I stand at the edge of the lake in our long skirts and long-sleeved shirts, and when the water surrounds our ankles it is sweetly cold.

Esty turns to me, grinning, and hikes her skirt. We walk into the water until our knees are submerged. The bottom is silty beneath our toes, slippery like clay, and tiny fish flash around our legs like sparks. We are forbidden to swim because it is immodest to show our bodies, but as far as I know there's no law against wading fully clothed. My cousin lets the hem of her skirt fall into the water and walks in all the way up to her waist, and I follow her, glad to feel water against my skin. This is the kind of thing we used to do when we were little—the secret sneaking-off into the woods, the accidental wrecking of our clothes, things we were punished for later. That was when Esty was still called Erica, before her parents got divorced, before she and her mother moved to Israel for a year and became Orthodox.

Now there is a new uncle, Uncle Shimon, and five little step-cousins. My Aunt Marla became Aunt Malka, and Erica became Esther. Erica used to talk back to her mother and throw bits of paper at the backs of old ladies' necks in synagogue, but in Israel she spent months repenting her old life and taking on a new one. This summer we've done nothing but pray, study Torah, cook, clean the lake cottage, and help Aunt Malka take care of the children. As we walk into the lake, I wonder if Erica still exists inside this new pious cousin.

I follow her deeper into the water, and the bottom falls away beneath us. It's hard to swim, heavy and slow, and at times it feels almost like drowning. Our denim skirts make it impossible to kick. Ahead is the Perelmans' old lake float, a raft of splintering boards suspended on orange plastic drums, and we pull hard all the way to the raft and hold on to the ladder.

"We're going to be killed when your mom sees our clothes,"
I say, out of breath.

"No, we won't," Esty says, pushing wet hair out of her face.
"We'll make up an excuse. We'll say we fell in."

"Yeah, right," I say. "Accidentally."

Far down below, at the bottom of the lake, boulders waver
in the blue light. It's exciting to think we've come this far in
skirts. The slow-moving shadows of fish pass beneath us, and
the sun is hot and brilliant-white. We climb onto the raft and
lie down on the splintering planks and let the sun dry our
clothes. It is good just to lie there staring at the cottage with
its sad vacant windows, no one inside to tell us what to do. In a
few more weeks I will go home to Manhattan, back to a life in
which my days are counted according to the American calendar
and prayer is something we do once a year, on the High
Holidays, when we visit my grandparents in Chicago.

Back in that other world, three hundred miles from here,
my mother lies in a hospital bed still recovering from the
birth and death of my brother. His name was Devon Michael.
His birth weight was one pound, ten ounces. My mother had
a problem with high blood pressure, and they had to deliver
him three months early, by C-section. It has been six weeks
since Devon Michael lived and died, but my mother is still in
the hospital, fighting infection and depression. With my

father working full-time and me out of school, my parents decided it would be better for me to go to the Adelsteins' until my mother was out of the hospital. I didn't agree, but it seemed like a bad time to argue.

My cousin says that when I go home I should encourage my parents to keep kosher, that we should always say b'rachot before and after eating, that my mother and I should wear long skirts and long-sleeved shirts every day. She says all this will help my mother recover, the way it helped her mother recover from the divorce. I try to tell her how long it's been since we've even done the normal things, like go to the movies or make a big Chinese dinner in the wok. But Esty just watches me with a distant enlightened look in her eyes and says we have to try to do what God wants. I have been here a month, and still I haven't told her any of the bad things I've done this year— sneaked cigarettes from my friends' mothers' packs, stole naked-lady playing cards from a street vendor near Port Authority, kissed a boy from swim team behind the bleachers after a meet. I had planned to tell her all these things, thinking she'd be impressed, but soon I understood that she wouldn't.

Now Esty sits up beside me on the raft and looks toward the shore. As she stares at the road beyond the Perelmans' yard, her back tenses and her eyes narrow with concentration. "Someone's coming," she says. "Look."

I sit up. Through the bushes along the lake road there is a flash of white, somebody's shirt. Without a word we climb down into the water and swim underneath the raft, between the orange plastic drums. From the lapping shade there we see a teenage boy with copper-colored hair and long curling peyos run from the road to the bushes beside the house. He drops to his knees and crawls through the tangle of vines, moving slowly, glancing back over his shoulder. When he reaches the backyard he stands and brushes dead leaves from his clothes. He is tall and lanky, his long arms smooth and brown. Crouching beside the porch, he opens his backpack and takes out some kind of flat package, which he pushes deep under the porch steps. Then he gets up and runs for the road. From the shadow of the raft we can see the dust rising, and the receding flash of the boy's white shirt.

"That was Dovid Frankel," Esty says.

"How could you tell?"

"My mother bought him that green backpack in Toronto."

"Lots of people have green backpacks," I say.

"I know it was him. You'll see. His family's coming for Shabbos tonight."

She swims toward shore and I follow, my skirt heavy as an animal skin around my legs. When we drag ourselves onto the beach our clothes cling to our bodies and our hair hangs like weeds.

"You look shipwrecked," I tell my cousin.

"So do you," she says, and laughs.

We run across the Perelmans' backyard to the screened-in porch. Kneeling down, we peer into the shadows beneath the porch steps. Planes of light slant through the cracks between the boards, and we can see the paper bag far back in the shadows. Esty reaches in and grabs the bag, then shakes its contents onto the grass. What falls out is a large softcover book called *Essence of Persimmon: Eastern Sexual Secrets for Western Lives.* On the cover is a drawing of an Indian woman draped in gold-and-green silk, reclining on cushions inside a tent. One hand disappears into the shadow between her legs, and in the other she holds a tiny vial of oil. Her breasts are high and round, her eyes tapered like two slender fish. Her lips are parted in a look of ecstasy.

"Eastern sexual secrets," Esty says. "Oh, my God."

I can't speak. I can't stop staring at the woman on the cover.

My cousin opens the book and flips through the pages, some thick with text, others printed with illustrations. Moving closer to me, she reads aloud: "One may begin simply by pressing the flat of the hand against the open yoni, allowing heat and energy to travel into the woman's body through this most intimate space."

"Wow," I say. "The open yoni."

Esty closes the book and stuffs it into the brown paper bag.

"This is obviously a sin," she says. "We can't leave it here. Dovid will come back for it."

"So?"

"You're not supposed to let your fellow Jew commit a sin."

"Is it really a sin?"

"A terrible sin," she says. "We have to hide it where no one will find it."

"Where?"

"In our closet at home. The top shelf. No one will ever know."

"But *we'll* know," I say, eyeing her carefully. Hiding a book like this at the top of our own closet is something Erica might have suggested, long ago.

"Of course, but we won't look at it," Esty says sternly, her brown eyes clear and fierce. "It's *tiuv,* abomination. God forbid anyone should ever look at it again."

My cousin retrieves her bike from the shed and stows the book between a bag of lettuce and a carton of yogurt. It looks harmless there, almost wholesome, in its brown paper sack. We get our bikes and ride for home, and by the time we get there our clothes are almost dry.

Esty carries the book into the house as if it's nothing, just another brown bag among many brown bags. This is the kind of ingenious technique she perfected back in her Erica days, and it works equally well now. Inside, everyone is too busy with Shabbos preparations to notice anything out of the ordinary. The little step-cousins are setting the table, arranging the Shabbos candles, picking up toys, dusting the bookshelves. Aunt Malka is baking challah. She punches down dough as she talks to us.

"The children need baths," she says. "The table has to be set. The Handelmans and the Frankels are coming at seven, and I'm running late on dinner, as you know. I'm not going to ask what took you so long." She raises her eyes at us, large sharp-blue eyes identical to my mother's, with deep creases at the corners and a fringe of jet-black lash. Unlike my mother she is tall and big-boned. In her former life she was Marla Vincent, a set dresser for the Canadian Opera Company in Toronto. Once I saw her at work, hanging purple velvet curtains at the windows in an Italian palazzo.

"Sorry we took so long," Esty says. "We'll help."

"You'd better," she says. "Shabbos is coming."

I follow my cousin down the hall and into our bedroom. On the whitewashed wall there is a picture of the Lubavitcher Rebbe, Menachem Schneerson, with his long steely beard and his eyes like flecks of black glass. He's on the east wall, the wall my cousin faces when she prays. His eyes seem to follow her as she drags the desk chair into the closet and stows *Essence of Persimmon* on the top shelf.

"What do we say to Dovid Frankel tonight?" I ask her.

"Nothing," she says. "We completely ignore him."

I make one last phone call to my mother before Shabbos. It's always frightening to dial the number of the hospital room because there's no telling what my mother will sound like when she answers. Sometimes she sounds like herself, quick and funny, and I can almost smell her olive-aloe soap. Other times, like today, she sounds just like she sounded when she told me Devon Michael had died.

"I can hardly hear you," she says, her own voice small and faint, somewhere far off down the line. The phone crackles with static.

"We went swimming today," I tell her, trying to speak loud. "It was hot."

Far away, almost too quiet to hear, she sighs.

"It's nearly Shabbos," I say. "Aunt Malka's baking challah."

"Is she?" my mother asks.

"How are you feeling?" I ask her. "When can you come home?"

"Soon, honey."

I have a sudden urge to tell her about the book we found, to ask her what we're supposed to do with something like that, to find out if she thinks it's a sin. I want to tell her about Dovid Frankel, how we saw him sneaking along the lake. I tell my mother things like this sometimes, and she seems to understand. But now she says to send her love to Aunt Malka and Uncle Shimon and Esty and all the step-cousins, and before I have a chance to really feel like her daughter again, we're already saying goodbye.

At six-thirty, the women and girls arrive. They bring steaming trays of potato kugel and berry cobbler, bottles of grape juice and sweet wine. The men are at shul, welcoming the Shabbos as if she were a bride, with the words *bo'i kallah*. Here the women do not go to synagogue on Fridays. Instead we arrange the platters of food and remove bread from the oven and fill cups with grape juice and wine. We are still working when the men and boys arrive, tromping through the kitchen and kissing their wives and daughters *good Shabbos*. My cousin, her hands full of raspberries, nudges me and nods toward a tall boy with penny-brown hair, and I know him to be Dovid Frankel, the boy from the lake, owner of *Essence of Persimmon*. I watch him as he kisses his mother and hoists his little sister onto his hip. He is tall and tanned, with small round glasses and a slender oval face. His mouth is almost girlish, bow-shaped and flushed, and his hair is close-cropped, with the exception of his luxuriously curled, shoulder-length peyos. He wears a collarless blue shirt in a fabric that looks homemade. I don't realize I'm staring at him until Esty nudges me again.

Everyone gathers around the dinner table, which we've set up on the screen porch. The men begin singing "Shalom Aleichem," swaying with the rise and fall of the melody. I feel safe, gathered in, with the song covering us like a prayer shawl and the Shabbos candles flickering on the sideboard. I pray for my mother and father. Dovid Frankel stands across from me, rocking his little sister as he sings.

Uncle Shimon, in his loose white Israeli shirt and embroidered yarmulke, stands at the head of the table. His beard is streaked with silver, and his eyes burn with a quick blue fire. As he looks around the table at his friends, his children, his new wife, I can tell he believes himself to be a lucky man. I think about my previous uncle, Walter, who has moved to Hawaii to do his astronomy research at a giant telescope there. Once he brought the family to visit us at Christmastime, and in his honor my mother set up a tiny plastic tree on our coffee table. That night we were allowed to eat candy canes and hang stockings at the fireplace, and in the morning there were silver bracelets for Esty and me, with our names engraved. Esty's bracelet said *Erica,* of course. I wonder if she still has it. I still have mine, though it is too small for me now.

Beside me, Esty looks down at her plate and fingers the satin trim at the waist of her Shabbos skirt. I catch her looking at Dovid Frankel, too, who seems oblivious to us both. From the bedroom, *Essence of Persimmon* exerts a magnetic pull I can feel in my chest. I watch Esty as we serve the soup and the gefilte fish, as we lean over Dovid Frankel's shoulder to replace his fork or remove his plates. My cousin's cheeks are flushed and her eyes keep moving toward Dovid, though sometimes they stray toward pregnant Mrs. Handelman, her belly swollen beneath the white cotton of her dress. Mrs. Handelman is Dovid Frankel's oldest sister. Her young husband, Lev, has a short blond beard and a nervous laugh. During the fish course, he tells the story of a set of false contractions that sent him and Mrs. Handelman running for the car. Mrs. Handelman, Esty whispers to me, is eighteen years old. Last year they went to school together.

We eat our chicken and kugel, and then we serve the raspberry cobbler for dessert. The little step-cousins run screaming around the table and crawl underneath. There is something wild and wonderful about the disorder of it all, a feeling so different from the quiet rhythms of our dinner table at home, with my mother asking me about my day at school and my father offering more milk or peas. Here, when everyone has finished eating, we sing the Birkat Hamazon. By now I know all the Hebrew words. It's strange to think that when I go home we will all just get up at the end of the meal and put our plates in the sink, without singing anything or thanking anyone.

When the prayer is over, my uncle begins to tell a story about the Belkins, a Jewish family some thirty miles up the lake whose house burned down in June. "Everything destroyed," he says. "Books, clothes, the children's toys, everything. No one was hurt, thank God. They were all visiting the wife's brother when it happened. An electrical short in the attic. So when they go back to see if anything can be salvaged, the only thing not completely burnt up is the mezuzah. The door frame? Completely burnt. But the mezuzah, fine. A little black, but fine. And so they send it to New York to have the paper checked, and you'll never believe what they find."

All the men and women and children look at my uncle, their mouths open. They blink silently in the porch light as if my uncle were about to perform some holy miracle.

"There's an imperfection in the text," my uncle says. "In the word *asher*. The letters aleph-shin are smudged, misshapen."

Young Mr. Handelman looks stricken. "Aleph-shin," he says. "Aish."

"That's right. And who knows what that means?" Uncle Shimon looks at each of the children, but the children just sit staring, waiting for him to tell them.

"I know," Dovid Frankel says. "It means fire."

"That's right," says Uncle Shimon. "Fire."

Around the table there is a murmur of amazement, but Dovid Frankel crosses his arms over his chest and raises an eyebrow at my uncle. "Aish," he says. "That's supposed to be what made their house burn down?"

My uncle sits back in his chair, stroking his beard. "A man has to make sure his mezuzah is kosher," he says. "That's his responsibility. Who knows how the letters got smudged? Was it the scribe, just being lazy? Was it his assistant, touching the text as he moved it from one worktable to another? Maybe a drop of water fell from a cup of tea the scribe's wife was bringing to her husband. Should we blame her?"

"For God's sake, don't blame the wife," my aunt says, and all the women laugh.

"I like to have our mezuzot checked every year," says my uncle. He leans back in his chair and looks at Dovid, crossing his fingers over his belly. "We alone are responsible for our relationship with Hashem. That's what Rebbe Nachman of Breslov taught us in the eighteenth century."

"We should have our mezuzah checked," Mr. Handelman

says, squeezing his wife's hand. He looks with worry at her swollen belly.

"I made a mezuzah at school," says one of the little step-cousins, a red-haired boy.

"You did not," his older brother says. "You made a mezuzah *cover*."

Esty and I get up to clear the dessert plates, and Dovid Frankel pushes his chair away from the table and stands. As we gather the plates, he opens the screen door and steps out into the night. My cousin shoots me a significant look, as if this proves that he has sinned against Hashem and is feeling the guilt. I take a stack of dessert plates into the kitchen, trying to catch a glimpse of Dovid through the window. But it is dark outside, and all I can see is the reflection of the kitchen, with its stacks of plates that we will have to wash. When the men's voices rise again, I go to the front of the house and step outside. The night is all around me, dew-wet and smelling like milkweed and pine needles and lake wind, and the air vibrates with cicadas. The tall grass wets my ankles as I walk toward the backyard. Dovid is kicking at the clothesline frame, his sneaker making a dull hollow *clong* against the metal post. He looks up at me and says, "Hello, Esty's cousin," and then continues kicking.

"What are you doing?" I ask him.

"Thinking," he says, kicking the post.

"Thinking what?"

"Does a smudged mezuzah make a family's house burn down?"

"What do you think?"

He doesn't answer. Instead he picks up a white stone from the ground and hurls it into the dark. We hear it fall into the grass, out of sight.

"Don't you believe in Hashem?" I ask him.

He squints at me. "Do *you*?"

"I don't know," I say. I stand silent in the dark, thinking about the one time I saw my brother before he died. He was lying in an incubator with tubes coming out of every part of his body, monitors tracing his breathing and heartbeat. His skin was transparent, his eyes closed, and all I could think was that he looked like a tiny skinny frog. Scrubbed, sterilized, gloved, I was allowed to reach in through a portal and touch his feverish skin. I felt terrible for him. *Get better, grow, kick,* I said to him silently. It was difficult to leave, knowing I might not see him again. But in the cab that night, on the way home with my father, I was imagining what might happen if he did live. The doctors had told us he could be sick forever, that he'd require constant care. I could already imagine my parents taking care of him every day, changing his tubes and diapers, measuring his tiny pulse, utterly forgetting about me. Just once, just for that instant, I wished he would die. If there is a God who can see inside mezuzahs, a God who burns people's houses for two smudged letters, then he must know that secret too. "Sometimes I hope there's not a God," I say. "I'm in a lot of trouble if there is."

"What trouble?" Dovid says.

"Bad trouble. I can't talk about it."

"Some people around here are scared of you," Dovid says. "Some of the mothers. They think you're going to show their kids a fashion magazine or give them an unkosher cookie or tell them something they shouldn't hear."

I have never considered this. I've only imagined the influence rolling from them to me, making me more Jewish, making me try to do what the Torah teaches. "I didn't bring any magazines," I tell him. "I've been keeping kosher all summer. I've been wearing these long-sleeved clothes. I can hardly remember what I'm like in my normal life."

"It was the same with your cousin," he says. "When she and your aunt first came here, people didn't trust them."

"I can't believe anyone wouldn't trust them," I say. "Or be scared of me."

"I'm not scared of you," he says, and reaches out and touches my arm, his hand cool and dry against my skin. I know he is not supposed to touch any woman who is not his mother or his sister. I can smell raspberries and brown sugar on his breath. I don't want to move or speak or do anything that will make him take his hand from my arm, though I know it is wrong for us to be touching and though I know he wouldn't be touching me if I were an Orthodox girl. From the house comes the sound of men laughing. Dovid Frankel steps closer, and I can feel the warmth of his chest through his shirt. For a moment I think he will kiss me. Then we hear a screen door bang, and he moves away from me and walks back toward the house.

That night, my cousin won't talk to me. She knows I was outside with Dovid Frankel, and this makes her furious. In silence we get into our nightgowns and brush our teeth and climb into bed, and I can hear her wide-awake breathing, uneven and sharp. I lie there thinking about Dovid Frankel, the way his hand felt on my arm, the knowledge that he was doing something against the rules. It gives me a strange rolling feeling in my stomach. For the first time I wonder if I've started to *want* to become the girl I've been pretending to be, whose prayers I've been saying, whose dietary laws I've been observing. A time or two, on Shabbos, I know I've felt a kind of holy swelling in my chest, a connection to something larger than myself. I wonder if this is proof of something, if this is God marking me somehow.

In the middle of the night, I wake to find Esty gone from her bed. The closet door is closed, and from beneath the door comes a thin line of light, the light we leave on throughout Shabbos. From inside I can hear a shuffling and then a soft thump. I get out of bed and go to the closet door. "Esty," I whisper. "Are you in there?"

"Go away," my cousin whispers back.

"Open up," I say.

"No."

"Do it now, or I'll make a noise."

She opens the closet door just a crack. I slide in. The book is in her hand, open to a Japanese print of a man and woman embracing. The woman's head is thrown back, her mouth open to reveal a sliver of tongue. The man holds her tiny birdlike hands in his own. Rising up from between his legs and entering her body is a plum-colored column of flesh.

"Gross," I say.

My cousin closes the book.

"I thought you said we were never going to look at it again," I say.

"We were going to ignore Dovid Frankel, too."

"So what?"

My cousin's eyes fill, and I understand: She is in love with Dovid Frankel. Things begin to make sense—our bringing the book home, her significant looks all evening, her anger. "Esty," I say. "It's okay. Nothing happened. We just talked."

"He was looking at you during dinner," she cries.

"He doesn't like me," I say. "We talked about you."

"About me?" She wipes her eyes with her nightgown sleeve.

"That's right."

"What did he say?"

"He wanted to know if you'd ever mentioned him to me," I lie.

"And?"

"I said you told me you went to school with his sister."

My cousin sighs. "Okay," she says. "Safe answer."

"Okay," I say. "Now you have to tell me what you're doing, looking at that book."

My cousin glances down and her eyes widen, as if she's surprised to find she's been holding the book all this time. "I don't know what I'm doing," she says. "The book was here. I couldn't sleep. Finally I just got up and started looking at it."

"It's a sin," I say. "That's what you told me before."

"I know."

"So let's go to bed, okay?"

"Okay," she says.

We stand there looking at each other. Neither of us makes a move to go to bed.

"Maybe we could just look at it for a little while," I say.

"A few minutes couldn't hurt," my cousin says.

This decides it. We sit down on the wooden planking of the closet floor, and my cousin opens the book to the first chapter. We learn that we are too busy with work, domestic tasks, and social activity to remember that we must take the time to respect and enjoy our physical selves and our partners' physical selves, to reap the benefits that come from regular, loving, sexual fulfillment. The book seems not to care whether "the East" means Japan, China, or India; the drawings show all kinds of Eastern people in sexual positions whose names sound like poetry: "Bamboo flute," "The Galloping Horse," "Silkworms Spinning a Cocoon." My cousin's forehead is creased in concentration as she reads, her eyebrows nearly meeting.

"What's the orgasm?" my cousin says. "They keep talking about the orgasm."

"I don't know," I say. "Check the index."

She flips to the index, and under *orgasm* there is a long list of page numbers. We choose one at random, page 83. My cousin reads in a whisper about how to touch oneself in order to achieve the word in question. We learn that one can use one's own fingers or any object whose shape and texture one finds pleasing, though the use of electronic vibrating devices is not recommended. These can cause desensitization, the book tells us. But certain Eastern devices, such as *ben wa* balls or the

String of Pearls, can greatly enhance a woman's pleasure.

"Sick," my cousin says.

"I still don't get it," I say.

"What do you think they mean by the *clitoris?*"

Though I have a vague idea, I find myself at a loss for words. My cousin looks it up in the index, and when she learns what it is she is amazed. "I thought that was where you peed from," she breathes. "How weird."

"It's weird, all right," I say.

Then she says, "I can't believe Dovid Frankel has read all this. His hands probably touched this page." She lets the book fall into her lap. It opens to a glossy drawing of a woman suspended in a swinglike contraption from the roof of a pavilion, high above a turbaned man who gazes up at her with desire and love. Two servants in long robes hold the cords that keep the woman suspended.

"Oh, my God," my cousin says, and closes the book. "We have to repent tomorrow, when we say Shacharit in the morning. There's a place where you can tell God what you did wrong."

"We'll repent," I say.

We stow the book on its high shelf and leave the closet. Our room is cold, the light coming in from outside a ghostly blue. We climb into our twin beds and say the Shema and the V'ahavta. The V'ahavta is the same prayer that's written in the text of a mezuzah, and when I say the word *asher* a sizzle of terror runs through me. Has God seen what we have just done? Are we being judged even now, as we lie in bed in the dark? I am awake for a long time, watching the cool air move the curtains, listening to the rushing of the grasses outside, the whir of the night insects. After some time I hear a change in the rhythm of breathing from my cousin's bed, and a faint rustle beneath the sheet. I pretend to be asleep, listening to the metallic tick of her bedsprings. It seems to go on for hours, connected with the sound of insects outside, the shush of grass, the wind.

The next morning I am the first to wake. I say the Shema and wash my hands in the basin we leave on the nightstand, cleansing myself as I open my eyes to this Shabbos morning. My cousin sleeps nearly sideways, her long legs hanging off the bed, covers pushed back, nightgown around her thighs. Though her limbs have not seen the sun all summer, her skin is a deep olive. There is a bruise on her knee the size of an egg, newly purple, which I know she must have gotten as we climbed the metal ladder onto the Perelmans' float. In her sleep her face is slack and flushed, her lips parted. It has never occurred to me that my cousin may be beautiful the way a woman is beautiful. With her cropped brown hair and full cheeks, she has always looked to me like a tall, sturdy child. But this morning, as she sleeps, there is a womanliness to her body that makes me feel young and unripe. I dress quietly so as not to wake her, and tiptoe out to the kitchen to find my uncle standing on the screen porch, beside the table, folding his tallis into its velvet bag so he can go to shul for morning services. Sunlight falls in through the screen and covers him with its gold dust. He is facing Jerusalem, the city where he and Aunt Malka found each other. I open the screen door and step out onto the porch.

"Rebecca," he says. "Good morning, good Shabbos." He smiles, smoothing his beard between both hands.

"Good Shabbos," I say.

"I'll be at Torah study this afternoon. After lunch."

"Okay."

"You look tired," he says. "Did you sleep?"

"I slept okay."

For a moment we stand looking at each other, my uncle still smiling. Before I can stop myself, I'm asking the question that pushes its way to the front of my mind. "After a person dies," I say, "is the family supposed to have the mezuzah checked?"

My uncle's hands fall from his beard. He regards me sadly, his eyes deep and grave. "When my first wife, Bluma Sarah, died," he says, "I had everything checked. Our mezuzah, my tefillin, our ketubah. The rebbe found nothing. finally I asked him to examine my soul, thinking I was the bearer of some imperfection. Do you know what the rebbe told me?"

"No," I say, looking at my feet, wishing I hadn't asked.

"He told me, 'Sometimes bad things just happen. You'll see why later. Or you won't. Do we always know why Hashem does what he does? *Neyn*.'"

"Oh."

"I think God wanted me to meet your aunt," says Uncle Shimon. "Maybe He wanted me to meet you, too." He tucks his tallis bag under his arm and buttons his jacket. "Bluma Sarah had a saying: *Der gleichster veg iz ful mit shtainer*."

"What's it mean?"

"The smoothest way is sometimes full of stones," he says.

All day I keep the Shabbos. This means I do not turn on a light or tear paper or write or bathe or cook or sew or do any of the thirty-nine kinds of work involved in building the Holy Temple. It is difficult to remember all the things one cannot do; as I sit in the tall grass, playing a clumsy round of duck-duck-goose with the little step-cousins, I am tempted to pull a grass blade and split it down its fibrous center, or weave a clover chain for one of the girls. But the Shabbos is all around us, in the quiet along the road and the sound of families in their yards, and I remember and remember all day. My cousin spends most of the day alone. I see her praying in a sunlit patch of yard, swaying back and forth as she reads from her tiny Siddur; then she lies in the grass and studies Torah. When she disappears into the house I follow her. She's closed herself into our closet again, the door wedged tight against intruders. I imagine her undoing this morning's work of repentance, learning new body-part names, new positions. When I whisper through the door for her to come out, she tells me to go away.

All day I'm not allowed to use the telephone to call my mother. I walk around and around the yard, waiting for the sun to dip toward the horizon. Aunt Malka watches me from the porch, looking worried, and then she calls me over.

"What's all this pacing?"

"I'm keeping Shabbos," I say.

"You can keep it right here with me," she says, patting the step beside her.

I sit down. Before us the older children are trying to teach the younger ones how to do cartwheels. They fly awkward arcs through the long grass.

"Your mother sounds much better," she says. "You'll be going home soon."

"Probably," I say.

"There's a lady I know who lives near you," she says, "I'll give you her number. She and some other women run a mikveh near your house, on Twenty-second and Third."

"What's a mikveh?"

"It's a ritual bath," she says. "It cleans us spiritually. All women go. Men, too. Your mother should go when she gets out of the hospital. You can go with her, just to watch. It's lovely. You'll see." One of the little boys runs up and tosses a smooth black pebble into Aunt Malka's lap, then runs away, laughing. "We're commanded to go after childbirth," she says.

"Commanded by who?"

"By Hashem," she says, turning the pebble in her fingers. Through its center runs a translucent white ribbon of quartz.

"Even if the baby dies?" I ask her. "Do you have to go then?"

"Yes," she says. "Especially then. It's very important and beautiful. The bath is very clean, and this particular one is tiled all in pink. The women will help your mother undress and brush her hair, so the water will touch every part of her. Then she'll step down into the bath—it's very deep and large, like a Jacuzzi—until she's completely covered. They'll tell her what b'rachot to say. Then she'll be clean."

"Everyone's supposed to do this?" I ask her.

"We're commanded to," she says. "Adults, anyway. For women, it's every month unless we're pregnant. When I'm here

I do it right in the lake. There's a woman who had a special shed built on her property, and that's where we go in."

"What if my mother doesn't want to go?" I ask.

"If you tell her how important it is, I'm sure she'll go," she says, and hands me the black pebble. I rub it with my thumb, tracing the quartz.

My aunt gathers the little step-cousins for a walk down the lake road, smoothing their hair, retrieving their lost shoes, securing their *kippot* with metal clips. I imagine her walking into the lake, her dark curls spreading out behind her, and my skin prickles cold in the heat. When she invites me to come along on the walk, I tell her I will stay home. I lie down in the grass and watch her start off down the road, the little step-cousins circling her like honeybees.

Real bees weave above me through the grass, their bodies so velvety I want to touch them. For what feels like the first time all summer, I am alone. I rub the pebble with my thumb, imagining it to be a magic stone that will make me smaller and smaller in the tall grass. I shrink to the size of a garter snake, a leaf, a speck of dust, until I am almost invisible. There is a presence gathering around me, an iridescent light I can see through my laced eyelashes. I lie still against the earth, faint with dread, and I feel the planet spinning through space, its dizzying momentum, its unstoppable speed. It is God who makes the shadows dissolve around me. He sharpens the scent of clover. He pushes the bees past my ears, directs the sun onto my back until my skin burns through the cotton of my Shabbos dress. I want to know what He wants and do what He wants, and I let my mind fall blank, waiting to be told.

When three stars come into the sky, the family gathers for Havdalah. We stand in a circle on the grass outside, all nine of us, and we light the braided candle and sing to God, thanking Him for creating fire, *aish*. According to the tradition, we examine our fingernails in the light of that candle, to remind us of the ways God causes us to grow. Then we smell spices and drink wine for a sweet week, and finally we sing the song about Eliyahu Hanavi, the prophet who will arrive someday soon to bring the Messiah. I stand with one arm around a little step-cousin and the other around Esty. As Havdalah ends she drifts off toward the house, one hand trailing through the long grass.

Now that Shabbos is over, the first thing I do is call my mother. Standing in the kitchen, I watch my aunt and uncle carrying children toward the house as I dial. For the first time it occurs to me that it might be awful for my mother always to hear children in the background when I call her, and I wonder if I should wait until they go to bed. But by that time the phone's ringing, and it's my father who answers anyway.

"Hey, son," he says. It's an old game between us; he calls me *son* and I call him *Pa,* like in the Old West. This is the first time we've done it since Devon Michael was born, though, and it sounds different now.

"Hi, Pa," I say, playing the game even so, because I miss him.

"Still out on the range?"

"Indeedy."

"How's the grub?"

"Grub's not bad," I say. "How's Ma?"

He sighs. "Sleeping."

"Not good?" I say.

"I think she needs you home," he says. "She's not feeling well enough now to do much, but I'll bet if she saw her kid she'd shape up pretty fast."

"When can I come home?"

"It looks like a couple of weeks," he says. "She's had some problems. Nothing serious, but the doctor thinks she might need IV antibiotics for a little while still."

"Aunt Malka says she should go to a ritual bath," I say. "To get spiritually clean."

There's a silence on my father's end, and I wonder if I've said something wrong. In the background I hear a woman's voice on the intercom but I can't make out what she's saying. "You there, Dad?" I say.

"I'd like to talk to your aunt," he says. "If she's around."

Something about his tone gives me pause. Even though Aunt Malka's just a few steps away, talking quietly out on the screen porch with Uncle Shimon, I tell my father she's gone out for milk. Silently I promise myself to repent this lie tomorrow, during Shacharit.

I can hear my father scratching his head, sharp and quick, the way he sometimes does. "You have her give me a call," he says. "All right?"

"All right," I say. "Tell Mom I love her."

He says he will.

That evening, my cousin disappears during dinner. We're all eating tomatoes and cottage cheese and thick slices of rye bread with whipped butter, the kind of meal we always eat after Shabbos, and in the middle of spreading my third slice of bread I look over and Esty's gone.

"Where's your cousin?" Aunt Malka says. "She didn't touch her food."

"I'll find her," I say. I go to our room and open the closet door, but the closet is empty. The book is gone from its high shelf. I glance around the room, and it takes me a few moments to see my cousin's huddled shape beneath her bedclothes.

"Esty," I say. "What are you doing?"

She lifts her head and looks at me, her cheeks flushed. In her hand she holds a flashlight. "Reading," she whispers.

"You can't just leave dinner," I say.

"I wanted to look something up."

"Your mom wants to know what's wrong."

"Tell her I have a headache," Esty says. "Say I took some aspirin and I'm lying down."

"You want me to lie?"

She nods.

"It's against the Ten Commandments."

Esty rolls her eyes. "Like you've never lied," she says.

"Maybe I don't anymore."

"Tonight you do," she says, and pulls the bedclothes over her head, rolling toward the wall. I go out to the dinner table and sit down, pushing at my slice of rye with a tomato wedge.

"Nu?" my aunt says. "What's the story?"

"She's reading," I say.

"In the middle of dinner?"

"It's all right," Uncle Shimon says. "Let her read. I wish some of these would read." He casts a hand over the heads of his own children.

"I read," says one of the little girls. "I can read the whole aleph-bet."

"That's right," her father says, and gives her another slice of bread.

I finish my dinner, and then it's left to me to do all the dishes while Aunt Malka bathes the step-cousins and gets them ready for bed. I stand there washing and looking out into the dark yard, seeing nothing, angry at my cousin and worried about her. I worry about my mother, too, lying in the hospital with intravenous antibiotics dripping into her arm, spiritually unclean. I've always assumed that my brother's death was some-how meant to punish *me,* since I was the one who imagined it in the first place, but now I wonder if we are all guilty. After all, we've been walking around doing exactly what we want, day in and day out, as if what God wants doesn't matter at all, as if God were as small and insignificant as the knickknacks on my grandmother's shelves, the porcelain swans and milkmaids we see when we go to her house for the High Holidays.

A thin strand of fear moves through my chest, and for a moment I feel faint. Then, as I look out the window, I see a white shape moving across the lawn, ghostly in the dark. I stare through the screen as the figure drifts toward the road, and when it hits the yellow streetlight glow I see it's my cousin.

Drying my hands on a dish towel, I run out into the yard. Esty is far away in the dark, but I run after her as fast as I can through the wet grass. When I get to the road she hears me coming and turns around.

"What are you doing?" I say, trying to catch my breath.

"Nothing," she says, but she's keeping one hand behind her back. I grab for the hand but she twists it away from me. I see she's holding a white envelope.

"What is it?" I say. "You're going to the post office in the middle of the night?"

"It's not the middle of the night."

"You snuck out," I say. "You don't have to sneak out just to mail a letter."

"Go inside," Esty says, giving me a little shove toward the house.

"No," I say. "I'm not going anywhere. I'll scream for your mother if you don't tell me what you're doing."

"You would," she says, "wouldn't you?"

I open my mouth as if to do it.

"It's a note to Dovid Frankel," she says. "It says if he wants to get his book back, he has to meet me at the Perelmans' tomorrow night."

"But you can't. It's forbidden."

"So what?" my cousin says. "And if you tell anybody about it, you're dead."

"You can't do anything to me."

"Yes I can," she says. "I can tell my mother this was *your* book, that you brought it from New York and have been trying to get us to read it."

"But she'll know you're lying," I say. "Dovid will tell her it's a lie."

"No he won't."

I know she's right. Dovid would never own up to the book. In the end he would think about how much he has to lose, compared to me. And so I stand there on the road, my throat tightening, feeling again how young I am and how foolish. Esty smooths the letter between her palms and takes a deep breath. "Now turn around," she says, "and go back into that house and pretend I'm in bed. And when I come back, I don't want to see you reading my book."

"*Your* book?" I say.

"Mine for now."

I turn around and stomp back toward the house, but when I get to the screen door I creep in silently. The little cousins are sleeping, after all. There is a line of light beneath my aunt and uncle's door, and I hear my uncle reading in Hebrew to Aunt Malka. I go to our bedroom and change into my nightgown and sit on the bed in the dark, trying to pray. The eyes of the Lubavitcher Rebbe stare down at me from the wall, old and fierce, and all I can think about is my cousin saying *You would, wouldn't you,* her eyes slit with spite. I brush my teeth and get into bed, and then I say the Shema. Saying it alone for the first time, I imagine myself back home in my own bed, whispering to God in the silence of my room, and the thought makes me feel so desolate I roll over and cry. But it isn't long before I hear Esty climbing through the window and then getting ready for bed, and even though I still feel the sting of her threat, even though I know she's ready to betray me, her presence is a comfort in the dark.

I struggle awake the next morning to find that Esty is already out of bed. From the kitchen I can hear the clink of spoons against cereal bowls and the high plaintive voices of the step-cousins. Aunt Malka's voice rises over theirs, announcing that today we will all go blueberry picking. I sigh in relief. Blueberry picking is what I need. I say the Shema and wash my hands in the basin beside the bed.

My cousin is in a fine mood today, her short bangs pulled back in two blue barrettes, a red bandanna at her throat. She sings in the van on the way to the blueberry farm, and all the little cousins sing with her. My aunt looks on with pleasure. At first I'm only pretending to have a good time, but then I find I no longer have to pretend. It feels good to swing a plastic bucket and make my slow way down a row of blueberry shrubs, feeling between the leaves for the sun-hot berries. My cousin acts as if nothing happened between us last night, as if we had never fought, as if she never went down the road to Dovid Frankel's house in the dark. When her pail is full she helps me fill my pail, and we both eat handfuls of blueberries, staining our shirts and skirts and skin.

Back at home the cousins study Torah with Uncle Shimon, and Aunt Malka and Esty and I bake blueberry cake. Esty keeps glancing at the clock, as if she might have to run out any minute to meet Dovid. When the telephone rings she gives a jolt, then lunges to pick it up.

"Oh, Uncle Alan," she says. "Hi."

Uncle Alan is my father. I stop stirring the cake batter and try to get the phone from my cousin, but she's already handing it to Aunt Malka.

"Hello, Alan," Aunt Malka says. I watch her face for bad news, but none seems to be forthcoming. "Yes," she says. "Yes. . . . Yes, we certainly are." Holding the phone between her cheek and shoulder, she walks out of the kitchen and into the little girls' bedroom and closes the door behind her.

"What's going on?" Esty says.

"I don't know." I pour cake batter into the floured pan Esty has prepared, and we slide it into the oven. Through the wall I can hear Aunt Malka's voice rising and falling. "I think it has to do with the mikveh," I say. "I told my dad yesterday that my mom should go, and he had a strange reaction."

"She does have to go," my cousin says. "You're supposed to go to the mikveh after you've given birth or had your period. Your husband can't touch you until you do."

"Your mom already told me that."

"There are hundreds of rules," she says, sighing. "Things we're supposed to do and not supposed to do. Maybe you'll learn about them when you're older."

"What rules?" I say. "I'm old enough."

"I can't just say them here in the kitchen."

"Yes, you can. What are the rules? What are you supposed to do?"

My cousin bends close to my ear. "You can't do it sitting or standing," she says. "You can't do it outside. You can't do it drunk. You can't do it during the day or with the lights on. You're supposed to think about subjects of Torah while you do it. Things like that."

"You're supposed to think about subjects of Torah?"

Esty shrugs. "That's what they say."

Through the wall we hear Aunt Malka's voice approaching, and my cousin moves away from me and begins wiping flour and sugar from the countertop. Aunt Malka comes out of the bedroom, her face flushed, her brows drawn together. She's already hung up the phone.

"How's my mother?" I ask her.

"Recovering," she says, gathering the cup measures and mixing bowls.

"Am I in trouble?"

"No." She sends hot water rolling into the sink and rubs soap into the dish sponge, then begins scrubbing a bowl. She looks as if she's the one who's been punished, her mouth drawn into a grim line. "You have to do what you think is right, Rebecca," she says, "even when the people around you are doing otherwise."

"Okay," I say.

"It's not a problem right now," she says, "but when you go home it may be."

I glance at Esty. She's looking at her mother intently. "Do you really believe that?" she says. "About doing what you think is right?"

"Absolutely," her mother says. "I've always told you that."

Esty nods, and Aunt Malka continues washing dishes, unaware of what she's just condoned.

At twelve-thirty that night my cousin dresses in a black skirt and covers her hair with a black scarf. She wraps *Essence of Persimmon* in its brown paper bag and tucks it under her arm.

The house is dark and quiet, everyone asleep.

"Don't do this, Esty," I whisper from my bed. "Stay home."

"If you tell anyone I'm gone, you're dead," she says.

"At least take me along," I say.

"You can't come along."

"Try and stop me."

"You know how I can stop you."

The dread eyes of the Lubavitcher Rebbe stare down at me from the wall. *Protect your cousin,* he seems to say, and though I don't know what I am supposed to protect her from, I climb out of bed and begin dressing.

"What are you doing?" Esty says.

"I'm coming along."

"This has nothing to do with you, Rebecca."

"I was with you when you found the book," I say.

Esty looks down at the brown paper bag in her hands. Her face, framed by the black scarf, is dark and serious. Finally she speaks. "You can come," she says. "But there's one condition."

"What condition?"

"If we get caught, you have to take the blame. You have to take the blame for everything."

"But that's not fair."

"That's the way it is," she says. "You decide."

We sit for a moment in the silence of our room. The curtains rise and fall at the window, beckoning us both into the night. "All right," I say.

"Get dressed, then," my cousin says. "We're already late."

I finish dressing. My cousin slides the bedroom window as far open as it will go, and we crawl out silently into the side yard. We creep through the grass and out to the road, where no cars pass at this time of night. When I look back, the house is pale and small. I imagine Bluma Sarah hovering somewhere above the roof, keeping watch, marking our progress toward the lake.

We walk in the long grass at the side of the road, keeping out of the yellow pools of light that spill from the streetlamps. In the grass there are rustlings, chatterings, sounds that make me pull my skirt around my legs and keep close to my cousin. We do not talk. The moon is bright overhead. The few houses we pass yield no sign of life. Tree frogs call in the dark, the rubber-band twang of their throats sounding to me like *God, God, God*. The road we walk is the same road we traversed on Friday afternoon, our bicycles heavy with Shabbos groceries. I can almost see the ghosts of us passing in the other direction, our faces luminous with the secret of the book, our clothes heavy and damp with lake water. Now we are different girls, it seems to me, carrying a different kind of weight.

By the time we emerge into the Perelmans' backyard, our

skirts are wet with dew. Our sneakers squelch as we tiptoe toward the screen porch. We pause in a stand of bushes, listening for Dovid Frankel, hearing nothing.

We wait. The hands on my cousin's watch read twelve fifty-five. The lake lies quiet against the shore like a sleeping animal, and the shadows of bats move across the white arc of the moon. At one o'clock we hear someone coming. We both suck in our breath, grab each other's arms. We see the shadow of Dovid Frankel moving across the dew-silvered lawn. We wait until he comes up, breathing hard, and sits down on the porch steps. Then we come out of the bushes.

Dovid jumps to his feet when he sees us. "Who's that?" he says.

"It's okay," my cousin whispers. "It's just us. Esty and Rebecca."

"Quiet," Dovid says. "Follow me."

We follow him up the steps and enter the moonlit darkness of the screen porch. For a long moment, no one says anything. It is utterly silent. All three of us seem to be holding our breath. Dovid looks at my cousin, then at me. "Where's my book?" he says.

Esty takes the brown paper bag from under her arm. She slides out *Essence of Persimmon*.

Dovid lets out a long sigh. "You didn't tell anyone, did you?"

"Are you kidding?" Esty says.

Dovid reaches for the book, but Esty holds it away from him.

"It's a sin," she says. "Looking at pictures like these. You know you're not supposed to do anything that would make you . . . that would give you . . ."

"That would make you do what?" Dovid says.

"I mean, look at these people," she says, stepping into a shaft of moonlight and opening the book. She takes Dovid's flashlight and shines it on a drawing of two lovers intertwined on an open verandah, watching tigers wrestle in the tiled courtyard. She stares at the drawing as if she could will herself into the scene, touch the lovers' garments, their skin, the tiles of the courtyard, the tigers' pelts.

"There are laws," my cousin says. "You can't just do it on a porch, with tigers there. You can't do it in a garden."

"I know," Dovid says.

"I'm serious," Esty says. She moves closer to Dovid. "There are rules for us. We have to be holy. We can't act like animals." She looks up at him, so close their foreheads are almost touching. "We can't have books like this."

"What do you want me to do?" he says. "What am I supposed to do?"

My cousin rises onto her toes, and then she's kissing Dovid Frankel, and he looks startled but he doesn't pull away. The book falls from her hand. Quietly I pick it up, and I open the screen door and step into the Perelmans' backyard. I walk through the long grass to the edge of the water and take off my shoes and socks. The water is warmer than the air, its surface still. I take one step into the lake, then another. I am all alone. I pull off my long-sleeved shirt and feel the night air on my bare skin. Then I step out of my skirt. I throw my clothes onto the shore, onto the grass. Still holding the book, I walk into the water and feel it on all parts of my body, warm, like a mouth, taking me gently in. When the sandy bottom drops away I float on my back, looking up at the spray of stars, at the dense gauze of the Milky Way. The moon spreads its thin white sheets across my limbs. In my hand the book is heavy with water, and I let it fall away toward the bottom.

Haiku

BASHŌ

TRANSLATED BY ROBERT HASS

Harvest moon—
walking around the pond
all night long.

A petal shower
of mountain roses,
and the sound of the rapids.

Cats making love—
when it's over, hazy moonlight
in the bedroom.

At the Lake

MARY OLIVER

A fish leaps
like a black pin—
then—when the starlight
strikes its side—

like a silver pin.
In an instant
the fish's spine
alters the fierce line of rising

and it curls a little—
the head, like scalloped tin,
plunges back,
and it's gone.

This is, I think,
what holiness is:
the natural world,
where every moment is full

of the passion to keep moving.
Inside every mind
there's a hermit's cave
full of light,

full of snow,
full of concentration.
I've knelt there,
and so have you,

hanging on
to what you love,
to what is lovely.
The lake's

shining sheets
don't make a ripple now,
and the stars
are going off to their blue sleep,

but the words are in place—
and the fish leaps, and leaps again
from the black plush of the poem,
that breathless space.

From *A Slender Thread: Rediscovering Hope at the Heart of Crisis*

DIANE ACKERMAN

Editor's Note: In *A Slender Thread*, Diane Ackerman writes about her experiences working as a counselor for a suicide prevention (SP) hotline. Here, she reflects on the bath, and its powers to cleanse and rejuvenate both body and mind.

So, as evening falls, I sink into the Jacuzzi in my bathroom. Both modern and pagan, it reminds me of ancient days, when hot baths were prescribed for depression, compulsiveness, mood swings, and other mental woes. Manic-depressives bathed in (and drank from) certain lithium-rich pools. Others chewed on willow bark for migraines. Steeping the flesh in hot water as if it were a bundle of tea leaves was a favorite cure for mental ills and heartbreaks alike. In the twentieth century, psychotherapy may have become the talking cure, but for centuries bathing was the water cure, and Europeans made regular pilgrimages to Bath, Baden-Baden, and a host of other spa towns to submerge in miracle waters bubbling up from the earth. The Romans before them doted on baths, and devised ingenious heating and plumbing systems, so that the bathhouse floors could be toasty, the steam rooms cleansing, and the mosaic-clad promenades a delight to bare feet. Bathhouses once offered Roman citizens an oasis—they were the perfect place for manicures, coiffures, massages, jugglers, conmen, flirtations, and gossip hounds—and an ideal spot to meditate on one's life and troubles.

We baptize with water, we purify with water, we take steam baths in small closeted clouds, we wash away the dirt and toil of the day with hot water, we dilute our food and drink with water, we stare for hypnotic hours at any abundance of water, be it aquarium or ocean, and we relax in a pool of water, especially if it has been heated to our own body temperature. We ourselves are contained estuaries, swamps, canals, and reefs. Women have monthly tides and wombs where eggs lie like roe. Small wonder the water world relaxes us. When we worship water we worship our own plumbing.

The other animals I share the yard with don't feel this way about water. Squirrels can swim, and many is the time I've seen one frantically treading water in the pool, unable to climb out until I've offered it a pole or broom to cling to. When they perch on the side of a green plastic tub to sip the fresh water I provide for them, they occasionally fall in and scramble back out again. Squirrels sometimes wash their faces with falling snowflakes. The deer drink from the stream in the woods, but they worry about deep water. The raccoons wash in shallow pools by moving their paws rapidly sideways, then they rub their faces with wet hands. I've seen a pheasant stand under a dripping tree limb to shower its feathers during a gentle rain. But by and large the animals don't wallow the way humans do.

There's the cheap and dirty wallow of a farm pond or a stream, there's the private wallow of a bath tub, and there's the high class and pricey wallow of a spa. The one that intrigues me most is at Bath in England. Although I've never submerged in its waters, I've sat beside them, plunged into them in my imagination, and often thought of the Saxon tribes who first settled the area around Bath and found the natural hot spring so astonishing that they swore a goddess produced it. Where did the water come from? It must have been an ancient rain that fell about 10,000 years ago and penetrated deep into the earth, rising when the water had been warmed by the heat of the earth's core. How miraculous hot water must have seemed to the ancients, even after the discovery of fire. It took so much fuel and labor to stoke a fire, haul water, and wait for it to boil. Hot water was rare, a luxury, and there it was day and night in flowing streams. Only a goddess could be responsible for such sensuous magic. The conquering Romans, lured by this liquid treasure, were frankly carnal about its value. But superstitious, too. The spring at Bath is full of curses—human curses. They were written on sheets of pewter and then thrown into the spring. We know many of the Roman bathers, their families, social life, and irritations only by the curses they left behind.

There are no curses or Roman mosaics in *my* bathroom, but it is a pleasuredome dedicated to the goddess of hot water. Heavily tiled in mauve, purple, lavender, and teal, it also includes two wallpaper designs that complement each other— a pattern taken from a Persian mosque, in teal, pale green, and lavender, and a peacock-feather pattern in lavender and teal. A broad border separates the two, combining their elements— large peacocks in full-tailed display alternating with fruitful trees of life. Two white sconces glow softly like ringed planets. I love this Garden of Allah retreat with its colorful flowerpot holding shampoos and a small birdbath (complete with pottery birds) filled with aromatherapy vials. Tiled benches flank the tub, one a window seat that looks out onto a flowerbed filled in summer with phlox, in spring with bushy yellow evening prim-rose, and in deep summer with tall snapdragons, blue balloon flowers, spidery pink gas flowers, tussocks of yellow coreopsis, and poker-tall purple liatris, miscellaneous lobelia, nasturtiums, and dahlias. I can also see the red flag on the mailbox through the window; the mailman's visit perpetually inspires hope and surprise in a two-writer household. Or I can watch the neighbor children bike in the cul-de-sac after school.

Some of SP's callers would profit from a good long soak in a hot fragrant tub, and from time to time I recommend that after we hang up they might consider brewing a cup of herb tea and steeping themselves in a tub of lavender or pine, two good spirit lifters. If they have apple-spice tea at home, I suggest this, since some researchers have found it successful in staving off panic attacks. I don't mention that, for ages, spas have been the main escape of melancholy women, who withdrew from family and society for a spell to take stock of their lives and let others serve and nourish them for a change. I don't tell them of the long tradition of women and baths, from the sacred cleansing baths of the ancient Hebrews (menstruating women were considered dirty) to the fashionable baths of eighteenth-century French women, who sometimes entertained while in the bath. Ben Franklin reports that his lady friend Madame Brillon received guests while bathing, with a board placed over her for modesty, although I'm not sure how she concealed her breasts. Eighteenth-century etiquette required many elegancies and protocols, and lovers too were bound by ornate rules of courtesy. A woman could receive socially while in bed or bath, because she and her visitors alike were expected to hide their feelings. Madame Brillon liked to set up a chess game on her bath board so that she and Ben could play flirtatious chess while other guests drifted in and out of the room.

I don't receive guests or play chess while in the tub, but I do have a board to lay across it, since I often work there. Indeed, I do most of my serious reading while partially submerged. I usually take food and drink with me, and also a portable phone, a pocket calendar, and a stack of good books. Two large skylights flood the room with sun and sky. Visitors often try to turn off the light, only to discover there's no light on—except the sun. Or they wonder at the dark luminosity on winter days when the skylights are covered in deep snow. But it's the twelve-inch Dynamax telescope on the tiled bench beside the tub that usually makes them twist their brows in surprise for a few moments, and then grin hugely. What better place to watch the moon and stars? The skylights turn the room into a peaceful observatory where, as Walt Whitman says:

> I open the scuttle at night and see the far-sprinkled systems,
> And all I see multiplied as high as I can cipher
>   edge but the rim of the farther systems
>
> Wider and wider they spread, expanding, always expanding,
> Outward and outward and forever outward.

Tonight, soaking in the clouds of pungent jasmine-scented bubbles, I tune in the moon as it floats overhead, and sight on the changing constellations and wandering planets. The moon is full. The man in the moon has his mouth rounded—I think he may be caroling. Leo floats by with a brilliant white roar. And then a parade of glittery stars, galaxies, and nebulae fills the telescope with images of distant worlds. In the dark, it's hard to tell where that field of stars begins and ends. Watching the stars veer through tight local orders and whirlwind tumults, I cup a handful of foam, smoothing it over one shoulder, and picture suns roiling down my back, galaxies clinging to my chest and arms, molten starblood trickling from an airborne knee. Planets rise up my neck. Seething in the small of my back, a stellar nursery whorls out neutron stars, black holes, vagabond comets. Suns cascade from each wrist, where my tiny pulse dislodges a thousand worlds. I can almost hear the crackling swan song of supernovae, the mournful whistle of pulsars, the disciplined panic of the newly born. Then, drenched in immortal quiet and a sandstorm of light, I lie back, so bristling with wonder that for long granite seconds I feel calm and contented, and would not have the universe be anything it is not.

The Nude Swim

ANNE SEXTON

On the southwest side of Capri
we found a little unknown grotto
where no people were and we
entered it completely
and let our bodies lose all
their loneliness.

All the fish in us
had escaped for a minute.
The real fish did not mind.
We did not disturb their personal life.
We calmly trailed over them
and under them, shedding
air bubbles, little white
balloons that drifted up
into the sun by the boat
where the Italian boatman slept
with his hat over his face.

Water so clear you could
read a book through it.
Water so buoyant you could
float on your elbow.
I lay on it as on a divan.
I lay on it just like
Matisse's *Red Odalisque.*
Water was my strange flower.
One must picture a woman
without a toga or a scarf
on a couch as deep as a tomb.

The walls of that grotto
were everycolor blue and
you said, "Look! Your eyes
are seacolor. Look! Your eyes
are skycolor." And my eyes
shut down as if they were
suddenly ashamed.

Loving

SALLIE BINGHAM

H arry and I are reading the last chapter of *Ulysses*—
the one we bought the book for, years ago, in Paris;
we are in the middle of Molly Bloom's yeses when
Harry starts to tell me about the sea cave and the girl.

Now, remember: Harry Mommoth and I have been married
for twenty-seven-and-a-half years, all anniversaries and birth-
days well-attended to; we have two daughters, aged twenty-five
and twenty-three, and two little granddaughters—women run
in my family, a fact with which Harry has easily made his peace.
He believes, I think, that we are all goddesses, or at least
goddesses-in-waiting, fertile with yeses, some held back will-
fully—just like Molly Bloom under the rhododendrons.

Harry launched into his story without preamble. "I found
the sea cave, on Crete. Then I went and hung around the youth
hostel in Athens until I saw a girl I wanted, and I took her back
there," he tells me.

"How old were you?" I instantly want to know. Harry, at
sixty-seven (we married late) has a face nearly destroyed by years
in the sun—he sails, skis, only began using sunblock five years

ago, under threat from his doctor—and even when I first knew him, his flimsy, flying hair was white. So I have spent half my life assembling Harry as he was, even though the few snapshots he's kept show nothing more than a shaggy boy.

"Twenty," he says. "It was the year I dropped out of Northwestern and bummed around Europe. I got lonely after six or seven months and decided to bed down on Crete. I planned to stay at least a month in the sea cave, with my pack and my sleeping bag. Nobody minded as far as I could tell."

"What was her name?"

He pretends not to remember, one of his kindly subterfuges. "Aurelia, Athena"—he has a liking for the *A*'s, perhaps because my name, Stella, is toward the other end of the alphabet.

"Oh, come on," I urge him past modesty.

"Sylvia," he admits. "From Cincinnati. She went back there, at the end of the month."

"The two of you stayed in the sea cave all that time?"

Harry doesn't answer at once. Sunday sunlight plays on the rim of my rosy teacup; *Ulysses* lies splayed on my knee. Under its weight my blue silk dressing gown—another of Harry's happy choices—is pressed out flat, and I can see the tip of my knee. We have been in bed all morning, and I am naked under the fluid silk.

"All that time," he says finally, daring to allow a little complacency in his voice.

"What did you do?"

"Fucked," he says, and now his satisfaction emerged, whole and glistening, like the freshly encapsulated bud of a purple iris.

I love his tales. I always want more.

"You had to eat now and then," I say, aiming for practicality, which cuts across my appetite in an unexpected way.

"There was a little trattoria—"

"Wrong country."

"Well, whatever. A little eatery on the cliff. We climbed up the path every morning at sunset, gorged ourselves on seafood, got drunk on ouzo, and tottered back down again."

"Not the best recipe for lovemaking."

"We were young. And I'm not sure I'd call it lovemaking."

I am still hungry for more details, but at the same time, he has given me enough. Harry fuels me in this way with his past, its array of astonishing images, as he fuels our little home industry—we make wooden toys—with his delightful designs, all variations on past themes: the woodchopper on Harry's windmill wears a pigtail and a beret, the puzzle princess is a brunette, although she still sleeps on seven mattresses, each of them an oblong piece, and under them all the round wooden pea.

"I think I'll rob you of that story," I say, and before I can get too excited by the thought, I go back to *Ulysses* and finish reading the chapter.

After that we are quiet for a while. Joyce's words flit around the room like trapped sparrows. There is suddenly not enough air—winter is dissolving into spring—and I get up with a groan (the chair near the fire is so comfortable) and open a window. Beyond our porch, the Jemez Mountains are still blazing with snow, but I know it is melting, running down the arroyos to the Rio Grande.

Harry wanders over and embraces me from behind. "What are you planning to do with my story?"

"Act it," I say as his arms tighten.

"That's a great idea."

In all our years together, only my timidity has held me back. For a while I wanted him to protest more, to try to hold me, but since I was cleaving to him from the beginning like a barnacle to a rock, his wanting or not wanting to hold me came to seem immaterial. I've been to Kenya, alone, and to India with a friend, and in both places I was following Harry's footsteps, although I tried to deny it.

"It's a good idea," I say, puffing up my courage. "I've never been to Crete. It's supposed to be full of wildflowers in the spring. I'll call Donna at Whirlwind Travel tomorrow, see what the airfare costs."

"The girls are coming next Sunday," he says neutrally, knowing there's no chance I've forgotten.

I do not feel the pang or the pull I expect, perhaps because he is holding me in his arms. "We'll have to put them off."

Again, his voice is neutral. "Susan and Sam started planning their trip to Italy last Christmas. They're depending on us to take the girls."

"I can't remember Christmas. Did it snow?"

"Stella, snow or no snow, you remember what you said." He does a not-entirely-kind imitation of my solicitous voice: "But we'd love to have the girls! It will be a treat for us! We never see them enough! Etcetera," he adds, unnecessarily.

"I meant it, then." I turn to face him, admiring, as I nearly always do, the glisten of his blue eyes in that flaming face. "But I've changed my mind, now. We'll just have to tell them."

He smiles, knowing I am as aware as he is of the utter unreality of such a plan. "They'll only be here two weeks."

I have nothing to say to that. After the girls' visit, there will be some other impediment. But it is not in me to remind him that we made our lives to accommodate other people: first, our daughters—and they were demanding enough, in their time; then my father, who wished, as he said, to die with us (he ended, instead, in an elegant old-age home, but that was after two years in our guest room); now our

149

granddaughters, as well as the financial and emotional needs of friends, who pass through our house and our lives, leaving those trampling, confusing footprints you see on old, muddy trails.

"I'm afraid we're stuck," Harry says, and I realize for the first time that he has never looked forward to the little girls' visit.

I decide to take a walk and think this over. I close the Joyce and put it on the shelf we reserve for first editions, then go up to put on my jeans. There are breakfast dishes to be washed and our tumbled bed to make, but I force myself to avoid them.

Outside, the rich smell of thawing earth buoys me up, and I remember myself as a tiny child, running along a sidewalk in Cleveland with a cherry lollipop stuck in my jaw.

Spring is always late here in the Rockies; the apricots are often pinched by an April frost, but I know I will be down in my garden before long, grubbing, my hands deep in the dirt.

I'll miss the first ground-breaking, though, and I won't be able to plant vegetable seeds as I usually do indoors under the grow-light Harry fixed for me, because I'll be in Crete living in Harry's sea cave.

I have rarely done anything that surprised anyone. My fierceness, such as it is, has always been attached to appropriate tasks: I fought to have my babies without anesthetic, then breast-fed them for a full year although my mother said breast-feeding was for peasants; I found progressive yet disciplined schools for them, and labored to be an effective parent and teacher, myself. My part-time jobs while the girls were growing up were all in and around schools and libraries. Now, in retirement, Harry and I have developed his woodcarving hobby into a profitable business. The little girls have a whole collection of our toys, although I suspect they prefer plastic. So my fierceness, such as it is, has always been used appropriately, to protect and enhance this delightful life.

And now I am going to Crete, to the sea cave.

I collect a handful of pinecones, newly emerged from the snow, to dry and use for our Sunday evening fire. We'll have a good cheese omelet, a salad, a half-bottle of white wine; we are careful about our diets, about indulgences generally, although I sometimes think our marriage is the greatest indulgence of all. At night we still sleep spoon-fashion, as we did during the early, hot years. Harry's skin against mine, his hand on my belly, his faint, white smell, are the only antidotes to my sleeplessness. Away from him, I hardly close my eyes.

I know what I am going to say when I get to the kitchen door. Inside, Harry is washing the breakfast dishes. "I'd like you to consider taking care of the girls so I can go."

He looks up, not startled, but plausible, smiling. "I'm not

real eager to do that."

"It's your chance." I sit down at the table, refold our napkins, elaborate. "You know when I'm around they always go to me. But they need you, Harry, and I think you need them, and with me out of the way, you'll be able to establish real relationships."

"With a three-year-old and a five-year-old?" For the first time, I detect a thread of anxiety in his voice. "You know I never had much in common with our girls until they reached the age of reason."

I remember his father, formidable even in old age, insisting that our daughters use a butter knife, not a table knife, to load their toast.

"This is your chance to change that pattern." I hardly know what I am saying, folding and refolding the soft, flowered napkins.

"I'm having a little trouble believing you mean this," Harry says.

"You've inspired me again, you should take part of the blame."

"Before, it was trips planned in advance, or learning to play the piano, or buying that scarlet dress."

"A lot of other things, too," I insist, although I am not up to making a list. "And your sea cave, unfortunately, is irresistible."

"Everything's changed. Crete certainly has. Probably there's a gate across the cave, and a guard, and a charge for going in."

"Then I'll find another. There must be a lot of them."

"You are nuts, you know that?" he says, coming over and taking hold of my hands. "I love you, and you are entirely nuts." And I realize that, finally, I have surprised him.

I go to the telephone. Talking to my oldest daughter, I detect artificiality in my voice. I sound like one of those handbooks that preach consciousness. I didn't know I was privy to this vocabulary.

To my surprise, Susan begins speaking the same tongue, and I remember that, for her generation, what we would have once called pure selfishness has a variety of names. "I think it's great," she says, "if you're sure Dad is up to taking care of the girls."

"He doesn't think he is, but of course he is," I babble, staring at the Audubon wild goose hanging on the wall. The glint in the eye of the goose seems, suddenly, malevolent. "Remember when I was sick that time? He took care of you and Louise, both, very competently."

"He had Annie doing everything practical," she reminds me.

"I'll have Mercedes here, I don't expect your father to change diapers."

"Clare has been toilet-trained for the past nine months," she says severely.

"Both girls know Mercedes from your visits. They love her!" I exclaim, perhaps a little too enthusiastically. "You and the husband-man can go to Rome and have a ball."

We share this joke title, since we both had the luck to marry uxorious men.

"Sounds like a great adventure, Mom," she says, signing off, and I remember that for her, too, the trip will be a first. "Just stay around long enough to get the girls settled, okay?"

That takes some time, several days, in fact; Clare, the younger girl, misses her mother and insists on sleeping with Harry and me, which we don't like but don't have the courage to resist. I begin to wonder whether she will sleep with Harry while I'm gone, and to imagine how she will be clinging to him by the time I come back; she is hardly old enough to hold me in her memory for two weeks. And the older girl is morose, staring out windows, asking about everything, even the cooking of hamburgers: "How long?"

But now Harry has the bit in his teeth—it seems he wants to claim these girls—and Donna at Whirlwind has found a relatively cheap fare for me. I am carried along on other people's determination that I will "have my dream," as Donna says, as though she knows me a good deal better than she does.

"Do you plan on being alone in the cave?" Harry asks the evening before I am to leave. He has drawn me a map that shows its location, on the south coast of the island.

"I don't favor hanging around youth hostels," I say, but I hear the equivocation in my voice.

"Take care of yourself, Stella," he says with a gentleness that brings tears to my eyes.

I detail all the steps I've taken to ensure that: my cell phone with its international capability, the typhoid shot my doctor didn't think I'd need until he heard where I planned to stay, the sturdy new backpack and top-quality lightweight sleeping bag I've bought. I even have new hiking boots, stout, with thickly-ridged soles. None of this, of course, means anything, but my display of all these wares allows us to end the evening peacefully.

Next morning, I'm off to the airport early, in the dark, before Harry wakes up.

On the flight to New York, I bury myself in the novel I've been trying to finish for months; alone, I don't read much, and with Harry I want to read everything out loud, which slows things down. So the four-hour flight is a luxury and a reprieve until we hit a storm west of the city and the plane begins to pitch.

I can't read anymore, and staring out the window at the armored clouds seems a mistake; the attendants have strapped themselves down, and the pilots are ominously silent. I want a word, a smile—and I turn to my seatmate, whom I have studiously avoided, and ask him to talk to me. He's a composed-looking Japanese gentleman, and his hand looks as light as a leaf; chatting, he lays it on mine, and the contact is reassuring. When we land safely I thank him, and then we go our separate ways.

I have a hotel room booked for the night on the upper East side, to be nearer to Kennedy in the morning. The hotel has the look of a European second-class hostelry, dignified and austere; I'm given a tiny, white bedroom facing a fire escape, and a bathroom dark and narrow as a shoe box.

Immediately I want to go out and walk the streets, which I do for an hour, astonished by the lushness of the goods on display in shop windows. But everything is closed, and it is late and wet; my hair, under my rain hat, has curled up tightly. Finally I go back to the tiny white bedroom and try without much success to sleep. I resist calling Harry because I know it will mean, eventually, saying good-bye.

In the morning I'm up early—my flight to Athens doesn't leave until late afternoon—and since my hotel has no restaurant, I hit the street. The rain has passed off during the night, leaving the gutters running with water; people are out, under umbrellas and raincoats, hurrying somewhere. I relish the luxury of having the whole day to myself, of being able to dawdle along the wet sidewalk. After a while I go into a little coffee-house, its window fogged by human breath.

A black woman is standing behind the high counter as though she is at the prow of a ship. She is grand, tall, solemn, her face shining in the dim light. Behind her the instruments of her trade are arrayed: bright, metallic espresso machines, silvery pitchers, dark square bags of coffee.

"Good morning," she says as I slide out of my raincoat. And she smiles.

It is her smile that tells me the truth of the situation: she is in charge here, she is someone to whom I owe obeisance.

"I don't know what to order," I tell her humbly because although I have been in many New York coffeehouses, this one has, suddenly, become a shrine.

"As damp and chilly as it is, I'd suggest a mocha," she says, going to work with her instruments. Her back is broad, powerful; even the skimpy, yellow uniform can't diminish it.

"I've never had a mocha," I tell her. She is surprised by this, asks where I come from, exclaims over the distance, listens with mild distraction to my commentary on my upcoming trip. When I tell her I plan to stay in a sea cave, she laughs, throwing back her head. "Where you get that idea?"

"My husband, years ago. He took a girl there."

She slides a sharp glance at me. "You going alone?"

"Yes," I say, and now I know I mean it.

Other people are coming in, ordering, settling themselves at small tables; I sit down at a shelf under the fogged window, sip my delicious mocha, and watch a bald man at the nearest table reading *The New York Times*. He is reading with great concentration, as though he is alone. I realize that I never read with that kind of concentration because I am occupied, entirely, by love.

I go back for another mocha and am a little disappointed when the black woman seems hardly to remember me; she is very busy now, I am a particle in her morning; she has assumed a larger shape in mine.

I think, suddenly, of calling Harry, and feel for my cell phone. It will still be early in the West, they will be asleep—the rosy baby girl probably tangled in Harry's arms. I put the phone away.

Later I go back to the hotel and sit in the small white bedroom, hardly denting the tightly-made bed. My gear is stacked in the corner—lumbering backpack, battered suitcase, conscientious-looking leather purse with everything that matters inside. I check my tickets and my passport for the fiftieth time, and notice that my face in the passport photo looks young and wan. I can't remember when the photo was taken—for what jaunt, real or imaginary? I go to the heavy-browed mirror to see how I look now, and my alert and sensitive, pale-blond face peers back at me as through mist.

Why am I in this hotel room? Where is it I think I'm going?

I take out my Greek guidebook, check for Harry's map, taped inside the cover, reread my itinerary, already soft from frequent foldings. I finger my traveler's checks, count the oddly-colored Greek bills Donna secured for me, pass my eyes over the little phrase book I've been studying for several days. All my tools are in place, as the black woman in the coffee-house has hers, carefully lined up, ready to be put into service. And yet my question isn't answered.

I sit on the bed for a long time. Sunlight slices through the window, separating the iron bars of the fire escape, and I remember the wooden hotels of my childhood, near Massachusetts beaches, with fire escapes scaling down their backs. Once, I climbed down a fire escape to meet a boy I was in love with; he caught me when I dropped the final eight feet to the ground, and we stood there, pressed together, unable to separate in the soft, sea-smelling night. It has always been like that for me: I have been deeply loved, I have loved deeply, and the service of my love has prepared me for what has seemed unwelcome in my life.

Harry, too, I realize, was prepared in the sea cave, all those years ago, as I have been prepared, once more, in the little coffeehouse, when the black woman smiled at me when I was drinking my first mocha, when I watched the bald man reading *The New York Times*—where nothing happened, and everything.

And so in the end I went home, not defeated, although Harry was alarmed, thinking I'd compromised.

Now, I am ready; and in the evening after the children are finally in bed, before their nightmares begin, and the distraction of consolation, I glance at Harry and see, crossing his reddened face, waves of reflected light from the blue Aegean, and I know that the same wave-light is crossing my face, scored by deepening lines, and that the light is then released into the infinite.

From *Seven Steps to Inner Power*

TAE YUN KIM

We cannot write in water. We cannot carve in water. Water's nature is to flow. And that is how we should treat negative emotion. When it comes, let it go. Let it flow away from you like water moving down a river bed.

How is this different from covering up an emotion? You acknowledge that you are feeling it, but immediately let it flow through and away from you. You do not deny it, but you release it.

A *Fundamentalist*

EDWARD HIRSCH

It was just a dump, really,
    a salt-sprayed room
        in a transient hotel
            falling into the open sea,

but we loved its tackiness—
    its crippled flamingos
        and blustering neon sign:
            Wellcome to U Travellers!

It was as if we had stepped
    over the edge
        of good taste
            onto a strange peninsula

remote beyond all reckoning
    where for three days
        and nights we went further
            and further into each other

and we did not turn back,

    we did not turn away.

        It was not a Revival meeting

            or a snake handling ceremony

but I'm not ashamed to say

    in that dingy room

        on the edge of nowhere

            I learned to pray, to become

a fundamentalist of your body.

    I don't know if I

        was lost or saved,

            but it was there, love,

I felt an angel's possessing

    grip, the flames

        rising from your skin,

            the shadow of the divine.

I knelt in a pentecostal church

    and spoke in tongues

        before I was lifted up

            and carried into the light.

River Music
from *Red: Passion and Patience in the Desert*

TERRY TEMPEST WILLIAMS

River. The river is brown is red is green is turquoise. On any given day, the river is light, liquid light, a traveling mirror in the desert.

Love this river, stay by it, learn from it. . . . It seemed to him that whoever understood this river and its secrets, would understand much more, many secrets, all secrets.

—*Siddhartha*

I love sitting by the river. A deep calm washes over me in the face of this fluid continuity where it always appears the same, yet I know each moment of the Rio Colorado is new.

"Have you learned that secret from the river; that there is no such thing as time?"

May 28, 2000—a relatively uneventful day. A few herons fly by, a few mergansers. Two rafts float through the redrock corridor. I wave. They wave back. One man is playing a harmonica, the oars resting on his lap as he coasts through flat water.

Sweet echoes continue to reach me.

I sit on the fine pink sand, still damp from high water days, and watch the river flow, the clouds shift, and the colors of the cliffs deepen from orange to red to maroon.

Present. Completely present. My eyes focus on one current in particular, a small eddy that keeps circling back on itself. Around and around, a cottonwood leaf spins; a breeze gives it a nudge, and it glides downriver, this river braided with light.

The eddy continues to coil the currents.

Boredom could catch up with me. But it never does, only the music, river music, the continual improvisation of water. Perhaps the difference between repetition and boredom lies in our willingness to believe in surprise, the subtle shifts of form that look large in a trained and patient eye.

I think about a night of lovemaking with the man I live with, how it is that a body so known and familiar can still take my breath all the way down, then rise and fall, the river that flows through me, through him, this river, the Colorado River keeps moving, beckoning us to do the same, nothing stagnant, not today, not ever, as my mind moves as the river moves.

"To find one's own equilibrium," he tells me this morning by the river. "That is what I want to learn."

He finds rocks that stand on their own and bear the weight

of others. An exercise in balance and form. Downriver, I watch him place a thin slab of sandstone on a rock pedestal, perfectly poised. He continues placing pebbles on top, testing the balance. In another sculpture, he leans two flat rocks against each other like hands about to pray.

The stillness of the stones, their silence, is a rest note against the music of the river.

Our shadows on the moving water are no different than those cast by the boulders on the bank. Composition. What is the composition of the river, these boulders, these birds, our own flesh? What is the composition of a poem except a series of musical lines?

River. River music. Day and night. Shadow and light. The roar and roll of cobbles being churned by the currents is strong. This river has muscle when flexed against stone, carved stone, stones that appear as waves of rock, secret knowledge known only through engagement. I am no longer content to sit, but stand and walk, walk to the river, enter the river, surrender my body to water now red, red is the Colorado, blood of my veins.

Sun

D. H. LAWRENCE

1

"Take her away, into the sun," the doctor said.

She herself was sceptical of the sun, but she permitted herself to be carried away, with her child, and a nurse, and her mother, over the sea.

The ship sailed at midnight. And for two hours her husband stayed with her, while the child was put to bed, and the passengers came on board. It was a black night, the Hudson swayed with heavy blackness, shaken over with spilled dribbles of light. She leaned over the rail, and looking down thought: this is the sea; it is deeper than one imagines, and fuller of memories. At that moment the sea seemed to heave like the serpent of chaos that has lived for ever.

"These partings are no good, you know," her husband was saying, at her side. "They're no good. I don't like them."

His tone was full of apprehension, misgiving, and there was a certain clinging to the last straw of hope.

"No, neither do I," she responded in a flat voice.

She remembered how bitterly they had wanted to get away from one another, he and she. The emotion of parting gave a slight tug at her emotions, but only caused the iron that had gone into her soul to gore deeper.

So, they looked at their sleeping son, and the father's eyes were wet. But it is not the wetting of the eyes that counts, it is the deep iron rhythm of habit, the year-long, life-long habits; the deep-set stroke of power.

And in their two lives, the stroke of power was hostile, his and hers. Like two engines running at variance, they shattered one another.

"All ashore! All ashore!"

"Maurice, you must go!"

And she thought to herself: For him it is All Ashore! For me it is Out to Sea!

Well, he waved his hanky on the midnight dreariness of the pier, as the boat inched away; one among a crowd. One among a crowd! C'est ça!

The ferry-boats, like great dishes piled with rows of lights, were still slanting across the Hudson. That black mouth must be the Lackawanna Station.

The ship ebbed on between the lights, the Hudson seemed interminable. But at last they were round the bend, and there was the poor harvest of lights at the Battery. Liberty flung up her torch in a tantrum. There was the wash of the sea.

And though the Atlantic was grey as lava, they did come at

last into the sun. Even she had a house above the bluest of seas, with a vast garden, or vineyard, all vines and olives, dropping steeply, terrace after terrace, to the strip of coast plain; and the garden full of secret places, deep groves of lemon far down in the cleft of earth, and hidden, pure green reservoirs of water; then a spring issuing out of a little cavern, where the old Sicules had drunk before the Greeks came; and a grey boat bleating, stabled in an ancient tomb with the niches empty. There was the scent of mimosa, and beyond, the snow of the volcano.

She saw it all, and in a measure it was soothing. But it was all external. She didn't really care about it. She was herself just the same, with all her anger and frustration inside her, and her incapacity to feel anything real. The child irritated her, and preyed on her peace of mind. She felt so horribly, ghastly responsible for him: as if she must be responsible for every breath he drew. And that was torture to her, to the child, and to everybody else concerned.

"You know, Juliet, the doctor told you to lie in the sun, without your clothes. Why don't you?" said her mother.

"When I am fit to do so, I will. Do you want to kill me?" Juliet flew at her.

"To kill you, no! Only to do you good."

"For God's sake, leave off wanting to do me good."

The mother at last was so hurt and incensed, she departed.

The sea went white, and then invisible. Pouring rain fell. It was cold, in the house built for the sun.

Again a morning when the sun lifted himself molten and sparkling, naked over the sea's rim. The house faced southeast, Juliet lay in her bed and watched him rise. It was as if she had never seen the sun rise before. She had never seen the naked sun stand up pure upon the sea-line, shaking the night off himself, like wetness. And he was full and naked. And she wanted to come to him.

So the desire sprang secretly in her, to go naked to the sun. She cherished her desire like a secret. She wanted to come together with the sun.

But she wanted to go away from the house—away from people. And it is not easy, in a country where every olive tree has eyes, and every slope is seen from afar, to go hidden, and have intercourse with the sun.

But she found a place: a rocky bluff, shoved out to the sea and sun, and overgrown with the large cactus called prickly pear. Out of this thicket of cactus rose one cypress tree, with a pallid, thick trunk, and a tip that leaned over, flexible, in the blue. It stood like a guardian looking to sea; or a candle whose huge flame was darkness against light: the long tongue of darkness licking up at the sky.

Juliet sat down by the cypress tree, and took off her clothes. The contorted cactus made a forest, hideous yet fascinating, about her. She sat and offered her bosom to the sun, sighing, even now, with a certain hard pain, against the cruelty of having to give herself: but exulting that at last it was no human lover.

But the sun marched in blue heaven and sent down his rays as he went. She felt the soft air of the sea on her breasts, that seemed as if they would never ripen. But she hardly felt the sun. Fruits that would wither and not mature, her breasts.

Soon, however, she felt the sun inside them, warmer than ever love had been, warmer than milk or the hands of her baby. At last, at last her breasts were like long white grapes in the hot sun.

She slid off all her clothes, and lay naked in the sun, and as she lay she looked up through her fingers at the central sun, his blue pulsing roundness, whose outer edges streamed brilliance. Pulsing with marvellous blue, and alive, and streaming white fire from his edges, the Sun! He faced down to her with blue body of fire, and enveloped her breasts and her face, her throat, her tired belly, her knees, her thighs and her feet.

She lay with shut eyes, the colour of rosy flame through her lids. It was too much. She reached and put leaves over her eyes. Then she lay again, like a long gourd in the sun, green that must ripen to gold.

She could feel the sun penetrating into her bones; nay, further, even into her emotions and her thoughts. The dark tensions of her emotion began to give way, the cold dark clots of her thoughts began to dissolve. She was beginning to be warm right through. Turning over, she let her shoulders lie in the sun, her loins, the backs of her thighs, even her heels. And she lay half stunned with the strangeness of the thing that was happening to her. Her weary, chilled heart was melting, and in melting, evaporating. Only her womb remained tense and resistant, the eternal resistance. It would resist even the sun.

When she was dressed again she lay once more and looked up at the cypress tree, whose crest, a filament, fell this way and that in the breeze. Meanwhile, she was conscious of the great sun roaming in heaven, and of her own resistance.

So, dazed, she went home, only half-seeing, sun-blinded and sun-dazed. And her blindness was like a richness to her, and her dim, warm, heavy half-consciousness was like wealth.

"Mummy! Mummy!" her child came running towards her, calling in that peculiar bird-like little anguish of want, always wanting her. She was surprised that her drowsed heart for once felt none of the anxious love-tension on return. She caught the child up in her arms, but she thought: He should not be such a lump! If he had any sun in him, he would spring up.—And she felt again the unyielding resistance of her womb, against him and everything.

She resented, rather, his little hands clutching at her, especially her neck. She pulled her throat away. She did not want him getting hold of it. She put the child down.

"Run!" she said. "Run in the sun!"

And there and then she took off his clothes and set him naked on the warm terrace.

"Play in the sun!" she said.

He was frightened and wanted to cry. But she, in the warm indolence of her body, and the complete indifference of her heart, and resistance of her womb, rolled him an orange across the red tiles, and with his soft, unformed little body he toddled after it. Then, immediately he had it, he dropped it because it felt strange against his flesh. And he looked back at her, wrinkling his face to cry, frightened because he was stark.

"Bring me the orange," she said, amazed at her own deep indifference to his trepidation. "Bring Mummy the orange."

"He shall not grow up like his father," she said to herself. "Like a worm that the sun has never seen."

2

She had had the child so much on her mind, in a torment of responsibility, as if, having borne him, she had to answer for his whole existence. Even if his nose were running, it had been repulsive and a goad in her vitals, as if she must say to herself: Look at the thing you brought forth!

Now a change took place. She was no longer vitally consumed about the child, she took the strain of her anxiety and her will from off him. And he thrived all the more for it.

She was thinking inside herself, of the sun in his splendour, and his entering into her. Her life was now a secret ritual. She always lay awake, before dawn, watching for the grey to colour to pale gold, to know if clouds lay on the sea's edge. Her joy was when he rose all molten in his nakedness, and threw off blue-white fire, into the tender heaven.

But sometimes he came ruddy, like a big, shy creature. And sometimes slow and crimson red, with a look of anger, slowly pushing and shouldering. Sometimes again she could not see him, only the level cloud threw down gold and scarlet from above, as he moved behind the wall.

She was fortunate. Weeks went by, and though the dawn was sometimes clouded, and afternoon was sometimes grey, never a day passed sunless, and most days, winter though it was, streamed radiant. The thin little wild crocuses came up mauve and striped, the wild narcissi hung their winter stars.

Every day, she went down to the cypress tree, among the cactus grove on the knoll with yellowish cliffs at the foot. She was wiser and subtler now, wearing only a dove-grey wrapper, and sandals. So that in an instant, in any hidden niche, she was naked to the sun. And the moment she was covered again she was grey and invisible.

Every day, in the morning towards noon, she lay at the foot of the powerful, silver-pawed cypress tree, while the sun strode jovial in heaven. By now she knew the sun in every thread of her body. Her heart of anxiety, that anxious, straining heart, had disappeared altogether, like a flower that falls in the sun, and leaves only a little ripening fruit. And her tense womb, though still closed, was slowly unfolding, slowly, slowly, like a lily bud under water it was slowly rising to the sun, to expand at last, to the sun, only to the sun.

She knew the sun in all her body, the blue-molten with his white fire edges, throwing off fire. And, though he shone on all the world, when she lay unclothed he focussed on her. It was one of the wonders of the sun, he could shine on a million people and still be radiant, splendid, unique sun, focussed on her alone.

With her knowledge of the sun, and her conviction that the sun was gradually penetrating her to know her in the cosmic carnal sense of the word, came over her a feeling of detachment from people, and a certain contemptuous tolerance for human beings altogether. They were so un-elemental, so un-sunned. They were so like graveyard worms.

Even the peasants passing up the rocky, ancient little road with their donkeys, sun-blackened as they were, were not sunned right through. There was a little soft white core of fear, like a snail in a shell, where the soul of the man cowered in fear of the natural blaze of life. He dared not quite see the sun: always innerly cowed. All men were like that.

Why admit men!

With her indifference to people, to men, she was not now so cautious about being seen. She had told Marinina, who went shopping for her in the village, that the doctor had ordered sun-baths. Let that suffice.

Marinina was a woman of sixty or more, tall, thin, erect, with curling dark-grey hair, and dark-grey eyes that had the shrewd-ness of thousands of years in them, with the laugh, half mockery, that underlies all long experience. Tragedy is lack of experience.

"It must be beautiful to go naked in the sun," said Marinina, with a shrewd laugh in her eyes, as she looked keenly at the other woman. Juliet's fair, bobbed hair curled in a little cloud at her temples. Marinina was a woman of Magna Graecia, and had far memories. She looked again at Juliet. "But when a woman is beau-tiful, she can show herself to the sun? eh? isn't it true?" she added, with that queer, breathless little laugh of the women of the past.

"Who knows if I am beautiful!" said Juliet.

But beautiful or not, she felt that by the sun she was appre-ciated. Which is the same.

When, out of the sun at noon, sometimes she stole down over the rocks and past the cliff-edge, down to the deep gully where the lemons hung in cool eternal shadow, and in the silence slipped off her wrapper to wash herself quickly at one of the deep, clear green basins, she would notice, in the bare green twilight under the lemon leaves, that all her body was rosy, rosy and turning to gold. She was like another person. She was another person.

So she remembered that the Greeks had said a white, unsunned body was unhealthy, and fishy.

And she would rub a little olive oil into her skin, and wander a moment in the dark underworld of the lemons, balancing a lemon-flower in her navel, laughing to herself. There was just a chance some peasant might see her. But if he did he would be more afraid of her than she of him. She knew the white core of fear in the clothed bodies of men.

She knew it even in her little son. How he mistrusted her, now that she laughed at him, with the sun in her face! She insisted on his toddling naked in the sunshine, every day. And now his little body was pink, too, his blond hair was pushed thick from his brow, his cheeks had a pomegranate scarlet, in the delicate gold of the sunny skin. He was bonny and healthy, and the servants, loving his gold and red and blue, called him an angel from heaven.

But he mistrusted his mother: she laughed at him. And she saw, in his wide blue eyes, under the little frown, that centre of fear, misgiving, which she believed was at the centre of all male eyes, now. She called it fear of the sun. And her womb stayed shut against all men, sun-fearers.

"He fears the sun," she would say to herself, looking down into the eyes of the child.

And as she watched him toddling, swaying, tumbling in the sunshine, making his little bird-like noises, she saw that he held himself tight and hidden from the sun, inside himself, and his balance was clumsy, his movements a little gross. His spirit was like a snail in a shell, in a damp, cold crevice inside himself. It made her think of his father. She wished she could make him come forth, break out in a gesture of recklessness, a salutation to the sun.

She determined to take him with her, down to the cypress tree among the cactus. She would have to watch him, because of the thorns. But surely in that place he would come forth from the little shell, deep inside him. That little civilized tension would disappear off his brow.

She spread a rug for him and sat down. Then she slid off her wrapper and lay down herself, watching a hawk high in the blue, and the tip of the cypress hanging over.

The boy played with stones on the rug. When he got up to toddle away, she got up too. He turned and looked at her. Almost, from his blue eyes, it was the challenging, warm look of the true male. And he was handsome, with the scarlet in the golden blond of his skin. He was not really white. His skin was gold-dusky.

"Mind the thorns, darling," she said.

"Thorns!" re-echoed the child, in a birdy chirp, still looking at her over his shoulder, like some naked *putto* in a picture, doubtful.

"Nasty prickly thorns."

"Ickly thorns!"

He staggered in his little sandals over the stones, pulling at the dry mint. She was quick as a serpent, leaping to him, when he was going to fall against the prickles. It surprised even herself. "What a wild cat I am, really!" she said to herself.

She brought him every day, when the sun shone, to the cypress tree.

"Come!" she said. "Let us go to the cypress tree."

And if there was a cloudy day, with the tramontana blowing, so that she could not go down, the child would chirp incessantly: "Cypress tree! Cypress tree!"

He missed it as much as she did.

It was not just taking sunbaths. It was much more than that. Something deep inside her unfolded and relaxed, and she was given to a cosmic influence. By some mysterious will inside her, deeper than her known consciousness and her known will, she was put into connection with the sun, and the stream of the sun flowed through her, round her womb. She herself, her conscious self, was secondary, a secondary person, almost an onlooker. The true Juliet lived in the dark flow of the sun within her deep body, like a river of dark rays circling, circling dark and violet round the sweet, shut bud of her womb.

She had always been mistress of herself, aware of what she was doing, and held tense in her own command. Now she felt inside her quite another sort of power, something greater than herself, darker and more savage, the element flowing upon her. Now she was vague, in the spell of a power beyond herself.

3

The end of February was suddenly very hot. Almond blossom was falling like pink snow, in the touch of the smallest breeze. The mauve, silky little anemones were out, the asphodels tall in bud, and the sea was corn-flower blue.

Juliet had ceased to care about anything. Now, most of the day, she and the child were naked in the sun, and it was all she wanted. Sometimes she went down to the sea to bathe: often she wandered in the gullies where the sun shone in, and she was out of sight. Sometimes she saw a peasant with an ass, as he saw her. But she went so simply and quietly with her child; and the fame of the sun's healing power, for the soul as well as for the body, had already spread among the people; so that there was no excitement.

The child and she were now both tanned with a rosy-golden tan, all over. "I am another being," she said to herself, as she looked at her red-gold breasts and thighs.

The child, too, was another creature, with a peculiar, quiet, sun-darkened absorption. Now he played by himself in silence, and she need hardly notice him. He seemed no longer to notice when he was alone.

There was not a breeze, and the sea was ultramarine. She sat by the great silver paw of the cypress tree, drowsed in the sun, but her breasts alert, full of sap. She was becoming aware of an activity rousing in her, an activity which would bring another self awake in her. Still she did not want to be aware. The new rousing would mean a new contact, and this she did not want. She knew well enough the vast cold apparatus of civilization, and what contact with it meant; and how difficult it was to evade.

The child had gone a few yards down the rocky path, round the great sprawling of a cactus. She had seen him, a real gold-brown infant of the winds, with burnt gold hair and red cheeks, collecting the speckled pitcher-flowers and laying them in rows. He could balance now, and was quick for his own emergencies, like an absorbed young animal playing.

Suddenly she heard him speaking: *Look, Mummy! Mummy, look!* A note in his bird-like voice made her lean forward sharply.

Her heart stood still. He was looking over his naked little

shoulder at her, and pointing with a loose little hand at a snake
which had reared itself up a yard away from him, and was opening its mouth so that its forked, soft tongue flickered black like
a shadow, uttering a short hiss.

"Look, Mummy!"

"Yes, darling, it's a snake!" came the slow deep voice.

He looked at her, his wide blue eyes uncertain whether to be
afraid or not. Some stillness of the sun in her reassured him.

"Snake!" he chirped.

"Yes, darling! Don't touch it, it can bite."

The snake had sunk down, and was reaching away from the
coils in which it had been basking asleep, and slowly was easing
its long, gold-brown body into the rocks, with slow curves. The
boy turned and watched it in silence. Then he said:

"Snake going!"

"Yes! Let it go. It likes to be alone."

He still watched the slow, easing length as the creature drew
itself apathetic out of sight.

"Snake gone back," he said.

"Yes, it's gone back. Come to Mummy a moment."

He came and sat with his plump, naked little body on her
naked lap, and she smoothed his burnt, bright hair. She said
nothing, feeling that everything was passed. The curious careless
power of the sun filled her, filled the whole place like a charm,

and the snake was part of the place, along with her and the child.

Another day, in the dry stone wall of one of the olive terraces, she saw a black snake horizontally creeping.

"Marinina," she said, "I saw a black snake. Are they harmful?"

"Ah, the black snakes, no! But the yellow ones, yes! If the
yellow one bites you, you die. But they frighten me, they
frighten me, even the black ones, when I see one."

Juliet still went to the cypress tree with the child. But she
always looked carefully round, before she sat down, examining
everywhere where the child might go. Then she would lie and
turn to the sun again, her tanned, pear-shaped breasts pointing
up. She would take no thought for the morrow. She refused to
think outside the garden, and she could not write letters. She
would tell the nurse to write. So she lay in the sun, but not for
long, for it was getting strong, fierce. And in spite of herself, the
bud that had been tight and deep immersed in the innermost
gloom of her, was rearing, rearing and straightening its curved
stem, to open its dark tips and show a gleam of rose. Her womb
was coming open wide with rosy ecstasy, like a lotus flower.

4

Spring was becoming summer, in the south of the sun, and the
rays were very powerful. In the hot hours she would lie in the

shade of trees, or she would even go down to the depths of the cool lemon grove. Or sometimes she went in the shadowy deeps of the gullies, at the bottom of the little ravine, towards home. The child fluttered around in silence, like a young animal absorbed in life.

Going slowly home in her nakedness down among the bushes of the dark ravine, one noon, she came round a rock suddenly upon a peasant of the next *podere,* who was stooping binding up a bundle of brush-wood he had cut, his ass standing near. He was wearing summer cotton trousers, and stooping his buttocks towards her. It was utterly still and private down in the dark bed of the little ravine. A weakness came over her, for a moment she could not move. The man lifted the bundle of wood with powerful shoulders, and turned to the ass. He started and stood transfixed as he saw her, as if it were a vision. Then his eyes met hers, and she felt the blue fire running through her limbs to her womb, which was spreading in the helpless ecstasy. Still they looked into each other's eyes, and the fire flowed between them, like the blue, streaming fire from the heart of the sun. And she saw the phallus rise under his clothing, and knew he would come towards her.

"Mummy, a man! Mummy!" The child had put a hand against her thigh. "Mummy a man!"

She heard the note of fear and swung round.

"It's all right, boy!" she said, and taking him by the hand, she led him back round the rock again, while the peasant watched her naked, retreating buttocks lift and fall.

She put on her wrap, and taking the boy in her arms, began to stagger up a steep goat-track through the yellow-flowering tangle of shrubs, up the level of day, and the olive trees below the house. There she sat down to collect herself.

The sea was blue, very blue and soft and still-looking, and her womb inside her was wide open, wide open like a lotus flower, or a cactus flower, in a radiant sort of eagerness. She could feel it, and it dominated her consciousness. And a biting chagrin burned in her breast, against the child, against the complication of frustration.

She knew the peasant by sight: a man something over thirty, broad and very powerfully set. She had many times watched him from the terrace of her house: watched him come with his ass, watched him trimming the olive tress, working alone, always alone and physically powerful, with a broad red face and a quiet self-possession. She had spoken to him once or twice, and met his big blue eyes, dark and southern hot. And she knew his sudden gestures, a little violent and over-generous. But she had never thought of him. Save that she had noticed that he was always very clean and well-cared for: and then she had seen his wife one day, when the latter had brought the man's meal, and they sat in the shade of a carob tree, on either side the spread white cloth. And then Juliet had seen the man's wife was older than he, a dark, proud, gloomy woman. And then a young woman had come with a child, and the man had danced with the child, so young and passionate. But it was not his child; he had no children. It was when he danced with the child in such a sprightly way, as if full of suppressed passion, that Juliet had first really noticed him. But even then, she had never thought of him. Such a broad red face, such a great chest, and rather short legs. Too much a crude beast for her to think of, a peasant.

But now the strange challenge of his eyes had held her, blue and overwhelming like the blue sun's heart. And she had seen the fierce stirring of the phallus under his thin trousers: for her. And with his red face, and with his broad body, he was like the sun to her, the sun in its broad heat.

She felt him so powerfully, that she could not go further from him. She continued to sit there under the tree. Then she heard nurse tinkling a bell at the house, and calling. And the child called back. She had to rise and go home.

In the afternoon she sat on the terrace of her house, that looked over the olive slopes to the sea. The man came and went, came and went to the little hut on his *podere,* on the edge of the cactus grove. And he glanced again at her house, at her sitting on the terrace. And her womb was open to him.

Yet she had not the courage to go down to him. She was paralysed. She had tea, and sat still there on the terrace. And the man came and went, and glanced, and glanced again. Till the evening bell had jangled from the capuchin church at the village gate, and the darkness came on. And still she sat on the terrace. Till at last in the moonlight she saw him load his ass and drive it sadly along the path to the little road. She heard him pass on the stones of the road behind her house. He was gone—gone home to the village, to sleep, to sleep with his wife, who would want to know why he was so late. He was gone in dejection.

Juliet sat late on into the night, watching the moon on the sea. The sun had opened her womb, and she was no longer free. The trouble of the open lotus blossom had come upon her, and now it was she who had not the courage to take the steps across the gully.

But at last she slept. And in the morning she felt better. Her womb seemed to have closed again: the lotus flower seemed back in bud again. She wanted so much that it should be so. Only the immersed bud, and the sun! She would never think of that man.

She bathed in one of the great tanks away down in the lemon-grove, down in the far ravine, far as possible from the other wild gully, and cool. Below, under the lemons, the child was wading among the yellow oxalis flowers of the shadow, gathering fallen lemons, passing with his tanned little body into flecks of light, moving all dappled.

She sat in the sun on the steep bank in the gully, feeling almost free again, the flower drooping in shadowy bud, safe inside her.

Suddenly, high over the land's edge, against the full-lit pale blue sky, Marinina appeared, a black cloth tied round her head, calling quietly: *Signora! Signora Giulietta!*

Juliet faced round, standing up. Marinina paused a moment, seeing the naked woman standing alert, her sun-faded hair in a little cloud. Then the swift old woman came down the slant of the steep, sun-blazed track.

She stood a few steps, erect, in front of the sun-coloured woman, and eyed her shrewdly.

"But how beautiful you are, you!" she said coolly, almost cynically. "Your husband has come."

"What husband?" cried Juliet.

The old woman gave a shrewd bark of a little laugh, the mockery of the woman of the past.

"Haven't you got one, a husband, you?" she said, taunting.

"How? Where? In America," said Juliet.

The old woman glanced over her shoulder, with another noiseless laugh.

"No America at all. He was following me here. He will have missed the path." And she threw back her head in the noiseless laugh of women.

The paths were all grown high with grass and flowers and

nepitella, till they were like bird-tracks in an eternally wild place. Strange, the vivid wildness of the old classic places, that have known men so long.

Juliet looked at the Sicilian woman with meditating eyes.

"Oh, very well!" she said at last. "Let him come."

And a little flame leaped in her. It was the opening flower. At least he was a man.

"Bring him here? Now?" asked Marinina, her mocking smoke-grey eyes looking with laughter into Juliet's eyes. Then she gave a little jerk of her shoulders.

"All right! As you wish! But for him it is a rare one!"

She opened her mouth with a noiseless laugh of amusement, then she pointed down to the child, who was heaping lemons against his little chest. "Look how beautiful the child is? An angel from heaven. That certainly will please him, poor thing. Then I shall bring him."

"Bring him," said Juliet.

The old woman scrambled rapidly up the track again and found Maurice at a loss among the vine terraces standing there in his grey felt hat and dark grey city suit. He looked pathetically out of place, in that resplendent sunshine and the grace of the old Greek world; like a blot of ink on the pale, sun-glowing slope.

"Come!" said Marinina to him. "She is down here."

And swiftly she led the way, striding with a long stride,

making the way through the grasses. Suddenly she stopped on the brow of the slope. The tops of the lemon trees were dark, away below.

"You, you go down here," she said to him, and he thanked her, glancing up at her swiftly.

He was a man of forty, clean-shaven, grey-faced, very quiet and really shy. He managed his own business carefully, without startling success, but efficiently. And he confided in nobody. The old woman of Magna Graecia saw him at a glance: he is good, she said to herself, but not a man, poor thing.

"Down there is the Signora," said Marinina, pointing like one of the Fates.

And again he said "Thank you! Thank you!" without a twinkle, and stepped carefully into the track. Marinina lifted her chin with a joyful wickedness. Then she strode off toward the house.

Maurice was watching his step, through the tangle of Mediterranean herbage, so he did not catch sight of his wife till he came round a little bend, quite near her. She was standing erect and nude by the jutting rock, glistening with the sun and with warm life. Her breasts seemed to be lifting up, alert, to listen, her thighs looked brown and fleet. Inside her, the lotus of her womb was wide open, spread almost gaping in the violet rays of the sun, like a great lotus flower. And she thrilled helplessly: a man was coming. Her glance on him, as he came gingerly, like ink on blotting-paper, was swift and nervous.

Maurice, poor fellow, hesitated, and glanced away from her, turning his face aside.

"Hello, Julie!" he said, with a little nervous cough. "Splendid! Splendid!"

He advanced with his face averted, shooting further glances at her furtively, as she stood with the peculiar satiny gleam of the sun on her tanned skin. Somehow she did not seem so terribly naked. It was the golden-rose of the sun that clothed her.

"Hello, Maurice!" she said, hanging back from him, and a cold shadow falling on the open flower of her womb. "I wasn't expecting you so soon."

"No," he said, "No! I managed to slip away a little earlier."

And again he coughed unawares. Furtively, purposely he had taken her by surprise.

They stood several yards away from one another, and there was silence. But this was a new Julie to him, with the sun-tanned, wind-stroked thighs: not that nervous New York woman.

"Well!" he said, "er—this is splendid, splendid! You are—er—splendid! Where is the boy?"

He felt, in his far-off depths, the desire stirring in him for the limbs and sun-wrapped flesh of the woman: the woman of flesh. It was a new desire in his life, and it hurt him. He wanted to side-track.

"There he is," she said, pointing down to where a naked urchin in the deep shade was piling fallen lemons together.

The father gave an odd little laugh, almost neighing.

"Ah, yes! There he is! So there's the little man! Fine!" His nervous, suppressed soul was thrilling with violent thrills, he clung to the straw of his upper consciousness. "Hello, Johnny!" he called, and it sounded rather feeble. "Hello, Johnny!"

The child looked up, spilling lemons from his chubby arms, but did not respond.

"I guess we'll go down to him," said Juliet, as she turned and went striding down the path. In spite of herself, the cold shadow was lifting off the open flower of her womb, and every petal was thrilling again. Her husband followed, watching the rosy, fleet-looking lifting and sinking of her quick hips, as she swayed a little in the socket of her waist. He was dazed with admiration, but also at a deadly loss. He was used to her as a person. And this was no longer a person, but a fleet sun-strong body, soulless and alluring as a nymph, twinkling its haunches. What would he do with himself? He was utterly out of the picture, in his dark grey suit and pale grey hat, and his grey, monastic face of a shy business man, and his grey mercantile mentality. Strange thrills shot through his loins and his legs. He was terrified, and he felt he might give a wild whoop of triumph, and jump towards that woman of tanned flesh.

"He looks all right, doesn't he," said Juliet, as they came through the deep sea of yellow-flowering oxalis, under the lemon trees.

"Ah!—yes! yes! Splendid! Splendid!—Hello, Johnny! Do you know Daddy? Do you know Daddy, Johnny?"

He squatted down, forgetting his trouser-crease, and held out his hands.

"Lemons!" said the child, birdily chirping. "Two lemons!"

"Two lemons!" replied the father. "Lots of lemons!"

The infant came and put a lemon in each of his father's open hands. Then he stood back to look.

"Two lemons!" repeated the father. "Come, Johnny! Come and say Hello! to Daddy."

"Daddy going back?" said the child.

"Going back? Well—well—not today."

And he gathered his son in his arms.

"Take a coat off! Daddy take a coat off!" said the boy, squirming debonair away from the cloth.

"All right, son! Daddy take a coat off."

He took off his coat and laid it carefully aside, then looked at the creases in his trousers, hitched them a little, and crouched down and took his son in his arms. The child's warm naked body against him made him feel faint. The naked woman looked down at the rosy infant in the arms of the man in his shirt sleeves. The boy had pulled off his father's hat, and Juliet looked at the sleek, black-and-grey hair of her husband, not a hair out of place. And utterly, utterly sunless! The cold shadow was over the flower of her womb again. She was silent for a long time, while the father talked to the child, who had been fond of his Daddy.

"What are you going to do about it, Maurice?" she said, suddenly.

He looked at her swiftly, sideways, hearing her abrupt American voice. He had forgotten her.

"Er—about what, Julie?"

"Oh, everything! About this! I can't go back into East Forty-Seventh."

"Er—" he hesitated, "no, I suppose not—Not just now, at least."

"Never!" she said, and there was a silence.

"Well—er—I don't know," he said.

"Do you think you can come out here?" she said savagely.

"Yes!—I can stay for a month. I think I can manage a month," he hesitated. Then he ventured a complicated, shy peep at her, and turned away his face again.

She looked down at him, her alert breasts lifted with a sigh, as if she would impatiently shake the cold shadow of sunlessness off her.

"I can't go back," she said slowly. "I can't go back on this sun. If you can't come here—"

She ended on an open note. But the voice of the abrupt, personal American woman had died out, and he heard the voice of the woman of flesh, the sun-ripe body. He glanced at her again and again, with growing desire and lessening fear.

"No!" he said. "This kind of thing suits you. You are splendid. No, I don't think you can go back."

And at the caressive sound of his voice, in spite of her, her womb-flower began to open and thrill its petals.

He was thinking visionarily of her in the New York flat, pale, silent, oppressing him terribly. He was the soul of gentle timidity in his human relations, and her silent, awful hostility after the baby was born had frightened him deeply. Because he had realized that she could not help it. Women were like that. Their feelings took a reverse direction, even against their own selves, and it was awful—devastating. Awful, awful to live in the house with a woman like that, whose feelings were reversed even against herself. He had felt himself borne down under the stream of her heavy hostility. She had ground even herself down to the quick, and the child as well. No, anything rather than that. Thank God, that menacing ghost-woman seemed to be sunned out of her now.

"But what about *you*?" she asked.

"I? Oh, I!—I can carry on the business, and—er—come over

here for long holidays—so long as you like to stay here. You stay as long as you wish—" He looked down a long time at the earth. He was so frightened of rousing that menacing, avenging spirit of womanhood in her, he did so hope she might stay as he had seen her now, like a naked, ripening strawberry, a female like a fruit. He glanced up at her with a touch of supplication in his uneasy eyes.

"Even for ever?" she said.

"Well—er—yes, if you like. For ever is a long time. One can't set a date."

"And I can do anything I like?" She looked him straight in the eyes, challenging. And he was powerless against her rosy, wind-hardened nakedness, in his fear of arousing that other woman in her, the personal American woman, spectral and vengeful.

"Er—yes!—I suppose so! So long as you don't make yourself unhappy—or the boy."

Again he looked up at her with a complicated, uneasy appeal—thinking of the child, but hoping for himself.

"I won't," she said quickly.

"No!" he said. "No! I don't think you will."

There was pause. The bells of the village were hastily clanging mid-day. That meant lunch.

She slipped into her grey crepe kimono, and fastened a broad green sash round her waist. Then she slipped a little blue shirt over the boy's head, and they went up to the house.

At table she watched her husband, his grey city face, his glued, black-grey hair, his very precise table manners, and his extreme moderation in eating and drinking. Sometimes he glanced at her furtively, from under his black lashes. He had the uneasy gold-grey eyes of a creature that has been caught young, and reared entirely in captivity, strange and cold, knowing no warm hopes. Only his black eye-brows and eye-lashes were nice. She did not take him in. She did not realize him. Being so sunned, she could not see him, his sunlessness was like nonentity.

They went on to the balcony for coffee, under the rosy mass of the bougainvillea. Below, beyond, on the next *podere,* the peasant and his wife were sitting under the carob tree, near the tall green wheat, sitting facing one another across a little white cloth spread on the ground. There was still a huge piece of bread—but they had finished eating and sat with dark wine in their glasses.

The peasant looked up at the terrace, as soon as the American emerged. Juliet put her husband with his back to the scene. Then she sat down, and looked back at the peasant. Until she saw his dark-visaged wife turn to look too.

5

The man was hopelessly in love with her. She saw his broad, rather short red face gazing up at her fixedly: till his wife turned to look, then he picked up his glass and tossed the wine down his throat. The wife stared long at the figures on the balcony. She was handsome and rather gloomy, and surely older than he, with that great difference that lies between a rather overwhelming, superior woman over forty, and her more irresponsible husband of thirty-five or so. It seemed like the difference of a whole generation. "He is my generation," thought Juliet, "and she is Maurice's generation." Juliet was not yet thirty.

The peasant in his white cotton trousers and pale pink shirt, and battered old straw hat, was attractive, so clean, and full of the cleanliness of health. He was stout and broad, and seemed shortish, but his flesh was full of vitality, as if he were always about to spring into movement, to work, even, as she had seen him with the child, to play. He was the type of Italian peasant that wants to make an offering of himself, passionately wants to make an offering of himself, of his powerful flesh and thudding blood-stroke. But he was also completely a peasant, in that he would wait for the woman to make the move. He would hang round in a long, consuming passivity of desire, hoping, hoping for the woman to come for him. But he would never try to advance to her: never. She would have to make the advance. Only he would hang round, within reach.

Feeling her look at him, he flung off his old straw hat, showing his round, close-cropped, brown head, and reached out with a large brown-red hand for the great loaf, from which he broke a piece and started chewing with bulging cheek. He knew she was looking at him. And she had such power over him, the hot, inarticulate animal, with such a hot, massive blood-stream down his great veins! He was hot through with countless suns, and mindless as noon. And shy with a violent, farouche shyness, that would wait for her with consuming wanting, but would never, never move towards her.

With him, it would be like bathing in another kind of sunshine, heavy and big and perspiring: and afterwards one would forget. Personally, he would not exist. It would be just a bath of warm, powerful life—then separating and forgetting. Then again, the procreative bath, like sun.

But would that not be good! She was so tired of personal contacts, and having to talk with the man afterwards. With that healthy creature, one would just go satisfied away, afterwards. As she sat there, she felt the life stemming from him to her, and her to him. She knew by his movements he felt her even more than she felt him. It was almost a definite pain of consciousness in the body of each of them, and each sat as if distracted, watched by a keen-eyed spouse, possessor. And Juliet thought: Why shouldn't I go to him! Why shouldn't I bear his child! It would be like bearing a child to the unconscious sun and the unconscious earth, a child like a fruit.—And the flower of her womb radiated. It did not care about sentiment or possession. It wanted man-dew only, utterly improvident.

But her heart was clouded with fear. She dare not! She dare not! If only the man would find some way! But he would not. He would only hover and wait, hover in endless desire, waiting for her to cross the gully. And she dare not. And he would hang round.

"You are not afraid of people seeing you when you take your sun-baths?" said her husband, turning round and looking across at the peasants. The saturnine wife over the gully, turned also to stare at the Villa. It was a kind of battle.

"No! One needn't be seen. Will you do it too? Will you take sun-baths?" said Juliet to him.

"Why—er—yes! I think I should like to, while I am here."

There was a gleam in his eyes, a desperate kind of courage of desire to taste this new fruit, this woman with rosy, sun-ripening breasts tilting within her wrapper. And she thought of him with his blanched, etiolated little city figure, walking in the sun in the desperation of a husband's rights. And her mind swooned again. The strange, branded little fellow, the good citizen, branded like a criminal in the naked eye of the sun. How he would hate exposing himself!

And the flower of her womb went dizzy, dizzy. She knew she would take him. She knew she would bear his child. She knew it was for him, the branded little city man, that her womb was radiating like a lotus, like the purple spread of a daisy anemone, dark at the core. She knew she would not go across to the peasant; she had not enough courage, she was not free enough.

And she knew the peasant would never come for her, he had the dogged passivity of the earth, and would wait, wait, only putting himself in her sight, again and again, lingering across her vision, with the persistency of animal yearning.

She had seen the flushed blood in the peasant's burnt face, and felt the jetting, sudden blue heat pouring over her from his kindled eyes, and the rousing of his big penis against his body—for her, surging for her. Yet she would never come to him—she daren't, she daren't, so much was against her.

And the little etiolated body of her husband, city-branded, would possess her, and his little, frantic penis would beget another child in her. She could not help it. She was bound to the vast, fixed wheel of circumstance, and there was no Perseus in the universe to cut the bonds.

Bilbo's Bath-Song

J.R.R. TOLKIEN

Sing hey! For the bath at close of day
that washes the weary mud away!
A loon is he that will not sing:
O! Water Hot is a noble thing!

O! Sweet is the sound of falling rain,
and the brook that leaps from hill to plain;
but better than rain or rippling streams
is Water Hot that smokes and steams.

O! Water cold we may pour at need
down a thirsty throat and be glad indeed;
but better is Beer, if drink we lack,
and Water Hot poured down the back.

O! Water is fair that leaps on high
in a fountain white beneath the sky;
but never did fountain sound so sweet
as splashing Hot Water with my feet!

TEXT CREDITS